FLIGHT FROM TOMORROW

SCIENCE FICTION STORIES

FLIGHT
FROM
TOMORROW

SCIENCE
FICTION
STORIES

by

H. BEAM
PIPER

CONTENTS

GRAVEYARD OF DREAMS

Standing at the armor-glass front of the observation deck and watching the mountains rise and grow on the horizon, Conn Maxwell gripped the metal hand-rail with painful intensity, as though trying to hold back the airship by force. Thirty minutes — twenty-six and a fraction of the Terran minutes he had become accustomed to — until he'd have to face it.

Then, realizing that he never, in his own thoughts, addressed himself as "sir," he turned.

"I beg your pardon?"

It was the first officer, wearing a Terran Federation Space Navy uniform of forty years, or about ten regulation-changes, ago. That was the sort of thing he had taken for granted before he had gone away. Now he was noticing it everywhere.

"Thirty minutes out of Litchfield, sir," the ship's officer repeated. "You'll go off by the midship gangway on the starboard side."

"Yes, I know. Thank you."

The first mate held out the clipboard he was carrying. "Would you mind checking over this, Mr. Maxwell? Your baggage list."

"Certainly." He glanced at the slip of paper. Valises, eighteen and twenty-five kilos, two; trunks, seventy-five and seventy kilos, two; microbook case, one-fifty kilos, one. The last item fanned up a little flicker of anger in him, not at any person, even himself, but at the situation in which he found himself and the futility of the whole thing.

"Yes, that's everything. I have no hand-luggage, just this stuff."

He noticed that this was the only baggage list under the clip; the other papers were all freight and express manifests. "Not many passengers left aboard, are there?"

"You're the only one in first-class, sir," the mate replied. "About forty farm-laborers on the lower deck. Everybody else got off at the other stops. Litchfield's the end of the run. You know anything about the place?"

"I was born there. I've been away at school for the last five years."

"On Baldur?"

"Terra. University of Montevideo." Once Conn would have said it almost boastfully.

The mate gave him a quick look of surprised respect, then grinned and nodded. "Of course; I should have known. You're Rodney Maxwell's son, aren't you? Your father's one of our regular freight shippers. Been sending out a lot of stuff lately." He looked as though he would have liked to continue the conversation, but said: "Sorry, I've got to go. Lot of things to attend to before landing." He touched the visor of his cap and turned away.

The mountains were closer when Conn looked forward again, and he glanced down. Five years and two space voyages ago, seen from the afterdeck of this ship or one of her sisters, the woods had been green with new foliage, and the wine-melon fields had been in pink blossom. He tried to picture the scene sliding away below instead of drawing in toward him, as though to force himself back to a moment of the irretrievable past.

But the moment was gone, and with it the eager excitement and the half-formed anticipations of the things he would learn and accomplish on Terra. The things he would learn — microbook case, one-fifty kilos, one. One of the steel trunks was full of things he had learned and accomplished, too. Maybe they, at least, had some value. . . .

The woods were autumn-tinted now and the fields were bare and brown.

They had gotten the crop in early this year, for the fields had all been harvested. Those workers below must be going out for the wine-pressing. That extra hands were needed for that meant a big crop, and yet it seemed that less land was under cultivation than when he had gone away. He could see squares of low brush among the new forests that had grown up in the last forty years, and the few stands of original timber looked like hills above the second growth. Those trees had been standing when the planet had been colonized.

That had been two hundred years ago, at the middle of the Seventh Century, Atomic Era. The name of the planet — Poictesme — told that: the Surromanticist Movement, when the critics and professors were rediscovering James Branch Cabell.

Funny how much was coming back to him now — things he had picked up from the minimal liberal-arts and general-humanities courses he had taken and then forgotten in his absorption with the science and tech studies.

The first extrasolar planets, as they had been discovered, had been named from Norse mythology — Odin and Baldur and Thor, Uller and Freya, Bifrost and Asgard and Niflheim. When the Norse names ran out, the discoverers had turned to other mythologies, Celtic and Egyptian and Hindu and Assyrian, and by the middle of the Seventh Century they were naming planets for almost anything.

Anything, that is, but actual persons; their names were reserved for stars. Like Alpha Gartner, the sun of Poictesme, and Beta Gartner, a buckshot-sized pink glow in the southeast, and Gamma Gartner, out of sight on the other side of the world, all named for old Genji Gartner, the scholarly and half-piratical adventurer whose ship had been the first to approach the three stars and discover that each of them had planets.

Forty-two planets in all, from a couple of methane-giants on Gamma to airless little things with one-sixth Terran gravity. Alpha II had been the only one in the Trisystem with an oxygen atmosphere and life. So Gartner had landed on it, and named it Poictesme, and the settlement that had grown up around the first landing site had been called Storisende. Thirty years later, Genji Gartner died there, after seeing the camp grow to a metropolis, and was buried under a massive monument.

Some of the other planets had been rich in metals, and mines had been opened, and atmosphere-domed factories and processing plants built. None of them could produce anything but hydroponic and tissue-culture foodstuffs, and natural foods from Poictesme had been less expensive, even on the planets of Gamma and Beta. So Poictesme had concentrated on agriculture and grown wealthy at it.

Then, within fifty years of Genji Gartner's death, the economics of interstellar trade overtook the Trisystem and the mines and factories closed down. It was no longer possible to ship the output to a profitable market in the face of the growing self-sufficiency of the colonial planets and the irreducibly high cost of space-freighting.

Below, the brown fields and the red and yellow woods were merging into a ten-mile-square desert of crumbling concrete — empty and roofless sheds and warehouses and barracks, brush-choked parade grounds and landing fields, airship docks, and even a spaceport. They were more recent, dating from Poictesme's second brief and hectic prosperity, when the Terran Federation's Third Fleet-Army Force had occupied the Gartner Trisystem during the System States War.

✳   ✳   ✳

Millions of troops had been stationed on or routed through Poictesme; tens of thousands of spacecraft had been based on the Trisystem; the mines and factories had reopened for war production. The Federation had spent trillions of sols on Poictesme, piled up mountains of stores and arms and equipment, left the face of the planet cluttered with installations.

Then, ten years before anybody had expected it, the rebellious System States Alliance had collapsed and the war had ended. The Federation armies had gone home, taking with them the clothes they stood in, their personal weapons and a few souvenirs. Everything else had been left behind; even the most expensive equipment was worth less than the cost of removal.

Ever since, Poictesme had been living on salvage. The uniform the first officer was wearing was forty years old — and it was barely a month out of the original packing. On Terra, Conn had told his friends that his father was a prospector and let them interpret that as meaning an explorer for, say, uranium deposits. Rodney Maxwell found plenty of uranium, but he got it by taking apart the warheads of missiles.

The old replacement depot or classification center or training area or whatever it had been had vanished under the ship now and it was all forest back to the mountains, with an occasional cluster of deserted buildings. From one or two, threads of blue smoke rose — bands of farm tramps, camping on their way from harvest to wine-pressing. Then the eastern foothills were out of sight and he was looking down on the granite spines of the Calder Range; the valley beyond was sloping away and widening out in the distance, and it was time he began thinking of what to say when he landed. He would have to tell them, of course.

He wondered who would be at the dock to meet him,

besides his family. Lynne Fawzi, he hoped. Or did he? Her parents would be with her, and Kurt Fawzi would take the news hardest of any of them, and be the first to blame him because it was bad. The hopes he had built for Lynne and himself would have to be held in abeyance till he saw how her father would regard him now.

But however any of them took it, he would have to tell them the truth.

The ship swept on, tearing through the thin puffs of cloud at ten miles a minute. Six minutes to landing. Five. Four. Then he saw the river bend, glinting redly through the haze in the sunlight; Litchfield was inside it, and he stared waiting for the first glimpse of the city. Three minutes, and the ship began to cut speed and lose altitude. The hot-jets had stopped firing and he could hear the whine of the cold-jet rotors.

Then he could see Litchfield, dominated by the Airport Building, so thick that it looked squat for all its height, like a candle-stump in a puddle of its own grease, the other buildings under their carapace of terraces and landing stages seeming to have flowed away from it. And there was the yellow block of the distilleries, and High Garden Terrace, and the Mall. . . .

At first, in the distance, it looked like a living city. Then, second by second, the stigmata of decay became more and more evident. Terraces empty or littered with rubbish; gardens untended and choked with wild growth; windows staring blindly; walls splotched with lichens and grimy where the rains could not wash them.

For a moment, he was afraid that some disaster, unmentioned in his father's letters, had befallen. Then he realized that the change had not been in Litchfield but in himself. After five years, he was seeing it as it really was. He wondered how his family and his friends would look to him now. Or Lynne.

The ship was coming in over the Mall; he could see the cracked paving sprouting grass, the statues askew on their pedestals, the waterless fountains. He thought for an instant that one of them was playing, and then he saw that what he had taken for spray was dust blowing from the empty basin. There was something about dusty fountains, something he had learned at the University. Oh, yes. One of the Second Century Martian Colonial poets, Eirrarsson, or somebody like that:

The fountains are dusty in the Graveyard of Dreams;
The hinges are rusty and swing with tiny screams.

There was more to it, but he couldn't remember; something about empty gardens under an empty sky. There must have been colonies inside the Sol System, before the Interstellar Era, that hadn't turned out any better than Poictesme. Then he stopped trying to remember as the ship turned toward the Airport Building and a couple of tugs — Terran Federation contragravity tanks, with derrick-booms behind and push-poles where the guns had been — came up to bring her down.

He walked along the starboard promenade to the gangway, which the first mate and a couple of airmen were getting open.

Most of the population of top-level Litchfield was in the crowd on the dock. He recognized old Colonel Zareff, with his white hair and plum-brown skin, and Tom Brangwyn, the town marshal, red-faced and bulking above the others. It took a few seconds for him to pick out his father and mother, and his sister Flora, and then to realize that the handsome young man beside Flora was his brother Charley. Charley had been thirteen when Conn had gone away. And there was Kurt Fawzi, the mayor of Litchfield, and there was Lynne, beside him, her red-lipped face tilted upward with a cloud of bright hair behind it.

He waved to her, and she waved back, jumping in excitement, and then everybody was waving, and they were pushing his family to the front and making way for them.

The ship touched down lightly and gave a lurch as she went off contragravity, and they got the gangway open and the steps swung out, and he started down toward the people who had gathered to greet him.

His father was wearing the same black best-suit he had worn when they had parted five years ago. It had been new then; now it was shabby and had acquired a permanent wrinkle across the right hip, over the pistol-butt. Charley was carrying a gun, too; the belt and holster looked as though he had made them himself. His mother's dress was new and so was Flora's — probably made for the occasion. He couldn't be sure just which of the Terran Federation services had provided the material, but Charley's shirt was Medical Service sterilon.

Ashamed that he was noticing and thinking of such things at a time like this, he clasped his father's hand and kissed his mother and Flora. Everybody was talking at once, saying things that he heard only as happy sounds. His brother's words were the first that penetrated as words.

"You didn't know me," Charley was accusing. "Don't deny it; I saw you standing there wondering if I was Flora's new boy friend or what."

"Well, how in Niflheim'd you expect me to? You've grown up since the last time I saw you. You're looking great, kid!" He caught the gleam of Lynne's golden hair beyond Charley's shoulder and pushed him gently aside. "Lynne!"

"Conn, you look just wonderful!" Her arms were around his neck and she was kissing him. "Am I still your girl, Conn?"

He crushed her against him and returned her kisses, assuring her that she was. He wasn't going to let it make a bit of difference how her father took the news — if she didn't.

She babbled on: "You didn't get mixed up with any of those girls on Terra, did you? If you did, don't tell me about it. All I care about is that you're back. Oh, Conn, you don't know how much I missed you . . . Mother, Dad, doesn't he look just splendid?"

Kurt Fawzi, a little thinner, his face more wrinkled, his hair grayer, shook his hand.

"I'm just as glad to see you as anybody, Conn," he said, "even if I'm not being as demonstrative about it as Lynne. Judge, what do you think of our returned wanderer? Franz, shake hands with him, but save the interview for the *News* for later. Professor, here's one student Litchfield Academy won't need to be ashamed of."

He shook hands with them — old Judge Ledue; Franz Veltrin, the newsman; Professor Kellton; a dozen others, some of whom he had not thought of in five years. They were all cordial and happy — how much, he wondered, because he was their neighbor, Conn Maxwell, Rodney Maxwell's son, home from Terra, and how much because of what they hoped he would tell them? Kurt Fawzi, edging him out of the crowd, was the first to voice that.

"Conn, what did you find out?" he asked breathlessly. "Do you know where it is?"

Conn hesitated, looking about desperately; this was no time to start talking to Kurt Fawzi about it. His father was turning toward him from one side, and from the other Tom Brangwyn and Colonel Zareff were approaching more slowly, the older man leaning on a silver-headed cane.

"Don't bother him about it now, Kurt," Rodney Maxwell scolded the mayor. "He's just gotten off the ship;

he hasn't had time to say hello to everybody yet."

"But, Rod, I've been waiting to hear what he's found out ever since he went away," Fawzi protested in a hurt tone.

Brangwyn and Colonel Zareff joined them. They were close friends, probably because neither of them was a native of Poictesme.

The town marshal had always been reticent about his origins, but Conn guessed it was Hathor. Brangwyn's heavy-muscled body, and his ease and grace in handling it, marked him as a man of a high-gravity planet. Besides, Hathor had a permanent cloud-envelope, and Tom Brangwyn's skin had turned boiled-lobster red under the dim orange sunlight of Alpha Gartner.

Old Klem Zareff never hesitated to tell anybody where he came from — he was from Ashmodai, one of the System States planets, and he had commanded a division that had been blasted down to about regimental strength, in the Alliance army.

"Hello, boy," he croaked, extending a trembling hand. "Glad you're home. We all missed you."

"We sure did, Conn," the town marshal agreed, clasping Conn's hand as soon as the old man had released it. "Find out anything definite?"

Kurt Fawzi looked at his watch. "Conn, we've planned a little celebration for you. We only had since day before yesterday, when the spaceship came into radio range, but we're having a dinner party for you at Senta's this evening."

"You couldn't have done anything I'd have liked better, Mr. Fawzi. I'd have to have a meal at Senta's before really feeling that I'd come home."

"Well, here's what I have in mind. It'll be three hours till dinner's ready. Suppose we all go up to my office in the meantime. It'll give the ladies a chance to go home and fix up for the party, and we can have a drink and a talk."

"You want to do that, Conn?" his father asked, a trifle doubtfully. "If you'd rather go home first . . ."

Something in his father's voice and manner disturbed him vaguely; however, he nodded agreement. After a couple of drinks, he'd be better able to tell them.

"Yes, indeed, Mr. Fawzi," Conn said. "I know you're all anxious, but it's a long story. This'll be a good chance to tell you."

Fawzi turned to his wife and daughter, interrupting himself to shout instructions to a couple of dockhands who were floating the baggage off the ship on a contra-gravity-lifter. Conn's father had sent Charley off with a message to his mother and Flora.

Conn turned to Colonel Zareff. "I noticed extra workers coming out from the hiring agencies in Storisende, and the crop was all in across the Calders. Big wine-pressing this year?"

"Yes, we're up to our necks in melons," the old planter grumbled. "Gehenna of a big crop. Price'll drop like a brick of collapsium, and this time next year we'll be using brandy to wash our feet in."

"If you can't get good prices, hang onto it and age it. I wish you could see what the bars on Terra charge for a drink of ten-year-old Poictesme."

"This isn't Terra and we aren't selling it by the drink. Only place we can sell brandy is at Storisende spaceport, and we have to take what the trading-ship captains offer. You've been on a rich planet for the last five years, Conn. You've forgotten what it's like to live in a poorhouse. And that's what Poictesme is."

"Things'll be better from now on, Klem," the mayor said, putting one hand on the old man's shoulder and the other on Conn's. "Our boy's home. With what he can tell us, we'll be able to solve all our problems. Come on, let's go up and hear about it."

They entered the wide doorway of the warehouse

on the dock-level floor of the Airport Building and crossed to the lift. About a dozen others had joined them, all the important men of Litchfield. Inside, Kurt Fawzi's laborers were floating out cargo for the ship — casks of brandy, of course, and a lot of boxes and crates painted light blue and marked with the wreathed globe of the Terran Federation and the gold triangle of the Third Fleet-Army Force and the eight-pointed red star of Ordnance Service. Long cases of rifles, square boxes of ammunition, machine guns, crated auto-cannon and rockets.

"Where'd that stuff come from?" Conn asked his father. "You dig it up?"

His father chuckled. "That happened since the last time I wrote you. Remember the big underground headquarters complex in the Calders? Everybody thought it had been all cleaned out years ago. You know, it's never a mistake to take a second look at anything that everybody believes. I found a lot of sealed-off sections over there that had never been entered. This stuff's from one of the headquarters defense armories. I have a gang getting the stuff out. Charley and I flew in after lunch, and I'm going back the first thing tomorrow."

"But there's enough combat equipment on hand to outfit a private army for every man, woman and child on Poictesme!" Conn objected. "Where are we going to sell this?"

"Storisende spaceport. The tramp freighters are buying it for newly colonized planets that haven't been industrialized yet. They don't pay much, but it doesn't cost much to get it out, and I've been clearing about three hundred sols a ton on the spaceport docks. That's not bad, you know."

Three hundred sols a ton. A lifter went by stacked with cases of M-504 submachine guns. Unloaded, one of them weighed six pounds, and even a used one was worth a hundred sols. Conn started to say something about that, but then they came to the lift and were crowding onto it.

He had been in Kurt Fawzi's office a few times, always with his father, and he remembered it as a dim, quiet place of genteel conviviality and rambling conversations, with deep, comfortable chairs and many ashtrays. Fawzi's warehouse and brokerage business, and the airline agency, and the government, such as it was, of Litchfield, combined, made few demands on his time and did not prevent the office from being a favored loafing center for the town's elders. The lights were bright only over the big table that served, among other things, as a desk, and the walls were almost invisible in the shadows.

As they came down the hallway from the lift, everybody had begun speaking more softly. Voices were never loud or excited in Kurt Fawzi's office.

Tom Brangwyn went to the table, taking off his belt and holster and laying his pistol aside. The others, crowding into the room, added their weapons to his.

That was something else Conn was seeing with new eyes. It had been five years since he had carried a gun and he was wondering why any of them bothered. A gun was what a boy put on to show that he had reached manhood, and a man carried for the rest of his life out of habit.

Why, there wouldn't be a shooting a year in Litchfield, if you didn't count the farm tramps and drifters, who kept to the lower level or camped in the empty buildings at the edge of town. Or maybe that was it; maybe Litchfield was peaceful because everybody was armed. It certainly wasn't because of anything the Planetary Government at Storisende did to maintain order.

After divesting himself of his gun, Tom Brangwyn took over the bartending, getting out glasses and filling a pitcher of brandy from a keg in the corner.

"Everybody supplied?" Fawzi was asking. "Well, let's drink to our returned emissary. We're all anxious to hear what you found out, Conn. Gentlemen, here's to our friend Conn Maxwell. Welcome home, Conn!"

"Well, it's wonderful to be back, Mr. Fawzi —"

"No, let's not have any of this mister foolishness! You're one of the gang now. And drink up, everybody. We have plenty of brandy, even if we don't have anything else."

"You telling us, Kurt?" somebody demanded. One of the distillery company; the name would come back to Conn in a moment. "When this crop gets pressed and fermented —"

"When I start pressing, I don't know where in Gehenna I'm going to vat the stuff till it ferments," Colonel Zareff said. "Or why. You won't be able to handle all of it."

"Now, now!" Fawzi reproved. "Let's not start moaning about our troubles. Not the day Conn's come home. Not when he's going to tell us how to find the Third Fleet-Army Force Brain."

"You *did* find out where the Brain is, didn't you, Conn?" Brangwyn asked anxiously.

That set half a dozen of them off at once. They had all sat down after the toast; now they were fidgeting in their chairs, leaning forward, looking at Conn fixedly.

"What did you find out, Conn?"

"It's still here on Poictesme, isn't it?"

"Did you find out where it is?"

He wanted to tell them in one quick sentence and get it over with. He couldn't, any more than he could force himself to squeeze the trigger of a pistol he knew would blow up in his hand.

"Wait a minute, gentlemen." He finished the brandy, and held out the glass to Tom Brangwyn, nodding toward the pitcher. Even the first drink had warmed him and he could feel the constriction easing in his throat and the lump at the pit of his stomach dissolving. "I hope none of you expect me to spread out a map and show you the cross on it, where the Brain is. I can't. I can't even give the approximate location of the thing."

Much of the happy eagerness drained out of the faces around him. Some of them were looking troubled; Colonel Zareff was gnawing the bottom of his mustache, and Judge Ledue's hand shook as he tried to relight his cigar. Conn stole a quick side-glance at his father; Rodney Maxwell was watching him curiously, as though wondering what he was going to say next.

"But it is still here on Poictesme?" Fawzi questioned. "They didn't take it away when they evacuated, did they?"

Conn finished his second drink. This time he picked up the pitcher and refilled for himself.

"I'm going to have to do a lot of talking," he said, "and it's going to be thirsty work. I'll have to tell you the whole thing from the beginning, and if you start asking questions at random, you'll get me mixed up and I'll miss the important points."

"By all means!" Judge Ledue told him. "Give it in your own words, in what you think is the proper order."

"Thank you, Judge."

Conn drank some more brandy, hoping he could get his courage up without getting drunk. After all, they had a right to a full report; all of them had contributed something toward sending him to Terra.

"The main purpose in my going to the University was to learn computer theory and practice. It wouldn't do any good for us to find the Brain if none of us are able to use it. Well, I learned enough to be able to operate, program and service any computer in existence, and train assistants. During my last year at the University, I had a part-time paid job programming the big positron-neutrino-photon computer in the astrophysics department. When I graduated, I was offered a position as instructor in positronic computer theory."

"You never mentioned that in your letters, son," his father said.

"It was too late for any letter except one that would come on the same ship I did. Beside, it wasn't very important."

"I think it was." There was a catch in old Professor Kellton's voice. "One of my boys, from the Academy, offered a place on the faculty of the University of Montevideo, on Terra!" He poured himself a second drink, something he almost never did.

"Conn means it wasn't important because it didn't have anything to do with the Brain," Fawzi explained and then looked at Conn expectantly.

All right; now he'd tell them. "I went over all the records of the Third Fleet-Army Force's occupation of Poictesme that are open to the public. On one pretext or another, I got permission to examine the non-classified files that aren't open to public examination. I even got a few peeps at some of the stuff that's still classified secret. I have maps and plans of all the installations that were built on this planet — literally thousands of them, many still undiscovered. Why, we haven't more than scratched the surface of what the Federation left behind here. For instance, all the important installations exist in duplicate, some even in triplicate, as a precaution against Alliance space attack."

"Space attack!" Colonel Zareff was indignant. "There never was a time when the Alliance could have taken the offensive against Poictesme, even if an offensive outside our own space-area had been part of our policy. We just didn't have the ships. It took over a year to move a million and a half troops from Ashmodai to Marduk, and the fleet that was based on Amaterasu was blasted out of existence in the spaceports and in orbit. Hell, at the time of the surrender, we didn't have —"

"They weren't taking chances on that, Colonel. But

the point I want to make is that with everything I did find, I never found, in any official record, a single word about the giant computer we call the Third Fleet-Army Force Brain."

For a time, the only sound in the room was the tiny insectile humming of the electric clock on the wall. Then Professor Kellton set his glass on the table, and it sounded like a hammer-blow.

"Nothing, Conn?" Kurt Fawzi was incredulous and, for the first time, frightened. The others were exchanging uneasy glances. "But you must have! A thing like that —"

"Of course it would be one of the closest secrets during the war," somebody else said. "But in forty years, you'd expect *something* to leak out."

"Why, *during* the war, it was all through the Third Force. Even the Alliance knew about it; that's how Klem heard of it."

"Well, Conn couldn't just walk into the secret files and read whatever he wanted to. Just because he couldn't find anything —"

"Don't tell *me* about security!" Klem Zareff snorted. "Certainly they still have it classified; staff-brass'd rather lose an eye than declassify anything. If you'd seen the lengths our staff went to — hell, we lost battles because the staff wouldn't release information the troops in the field needed. I remember once —"

"But there *was* a Brain," Judge Ledue was saying, to reassure himself and draw agreement from the others. "It was capable of combining data, and scanning and evaluating all its positronic memories, and forming association patterns, and reasoning with absolute perfection. It was more than a positronic brain — it was a positronic supermind."

"We'd have won the war, except for the Brain. We had ninety systems, a hundred and thirty inhabited planets, a hundred billion people — and we were on the defensive in our own space-area! Every move we made was known and anticipated by the Federation. How could they have done that without something like the Brain?"

"Conn, from what you learned of computers, how large a volume of space would you say the Brain would have to occupy?" Professor Kellton asked.

Professor Kellton was the most unworldly of the lot, yet he was asking the most practical question.

"Well, the astrophysics computer I worked with at the University occupies a total of about one million cubic feet," Conn began. This was his chance; they'd take anything he told them about computers as gospel. "It was only designed to handle problems in astrophysics. The Brain, being built for space war, would have to handle any such problem. And if half the stories about the Brain are anywhere near true, it handled any other problem — mathematical, scientific, political, economic, strategic, psychological, even philosophical and ethical. Well, I'd say that a hundred million cubic feet would be the smallest even conceivable."

They all nodded seriously. They were willing to accept that — or anything else, except one thing.

"Lot of places on this planet where a thing that size could be hidden," Tom Brangwyn said, undismayed. "A planet's a mighty big place."

"It could be under water, in one of the seas," Piet Dawes, the banker, suggested. "An underwater dome city wouldn't be any harder to build than a dome city on a poison-atmosphere planet like Tubal-Cain."

"It might even be on Tubal-Cain," a melon-planter said. "Or Hiawatha, or even one of the Beta or Gamma planets. The Third Force was occupying the whole Trisystem, you know." He thought for a moment. "If I'd been in charge, I'd have put it on one of the moons of Pantagruel."

"But that's clear out in the Alpha System," Judge

Ledue objected. "We don't have a spaceship on the planet, certainly nothing with a hyperdrive engine. And it would take a lifetime to get out to the Gamma System and back on reaction drive."

Conn put his empty brandy glass on the table and sat erect. A new thought had occurred to him, chasing out of his mind all the worries and fears he had brought with him all the way from Terra.

"Then we'll have to build a ship," he said calmly. "I know, when the Federation evacuated Poictesme, they took every hyperdrive ship with them. But they had plenty of shipyards and spaceports on this planet, and I have maps showing the location of all of them, and barely a third of them have been discovered so far. I'm sure we can find enough hulks, and enough hyperfield generator parts, to assemble a ship or two, and I know we'll find the same or better on some of the other planets.

"And here's another thing," he added. "When we start looking into some of the dome-city plants on Tubal-Cain and Hiawatha and Moruna and Koshchei, we may find the plant or plants where the components for the Brain were fabricated, and if we do, we may find records of where they were shipped, and that'll be it."

"You're right!" Professor Kellton cried, quivering with excitement. "We've been hunting at random for the Brain, so it would only be an accident if we found it. We'll have to do this systematically, and with Conn to help us — Conn, why not build a computer? I don't mean another Brain; I mean a computer to help us find the Brain."

"We can, but we may not even need to build one. When we get out to the industrial planets, we may find one ready except for perhaps some minor alterations."

"But how are we going to finance all this?" Klem Zareff demanded querulously. "We're poorer than snakes, and even one hyperdrive ship's going to cost like Gehenna."

"I've been thinking about that, Klem," Fawzi said. "If we can find material at these shipyards Conn knows about, most of our expense will be labor. Well, haven't we ten workmen competing for every job? They don't really need money, only the things money can buy. We can raise food on the farms and provide whatever else they need out of Federation supplies."

"Sure. As soon as it gets around that we're really trying to do something about this, everybody'll want in on it," Tom Brangwyn predicted.

"And I have no doubt that the Planetary Government at Storisende will give us assistance, once we show that this is a practical and productive enterprise," Judge Ledue put in. "I have some slight influence with the President and —"

"I'm not too sure we want the Government getting into this," Kurt Fawzi replied. "Give them half a chance and that gang at Storisende'll squeeze us right out."

"We can handle this ourselves," Brangwyn agreed. "And when we get some kind of a ship and get out to the other two systems, or even just to Tubal-Cain or Hiawatha, first thing you know, we'll *be* the Planetary Government."

"Well, now, Tom," Fawzi began piously, "the Brain is too big a thing for a few of us to try to monopolize; it'll be for all Poictesme. Of course, it's only proper that we, who are making the effort to locate it, should have the direction of that effort. . . ."

While Fawzi was talking, Rodney Maxwell went to the table, rummaged his pistol out of the pile and buckled it on. The mayor stopped short.

"You leaving us, Rod?"

"Yes, it's getting late. Conn and I are going for a little walk; we'll be at Senta's in half an hour. The fresh air do both of us good and we have a lot to talk about. After all, we haven't seen each other for over five years."

✳   ✳   ✳

They were silent, however, until they were away from the Airport Building and walking along High Garden Terrace in the direction of the Mall. Conn was glad; his own thoughts were weighing too heavily within him: I didn't do it. I was going to do it; every minute, I was going to do it, and I didn't, and now it's too late.

"That was quite a talk you gave them, son," his father said. "They believed every word of it. A couple of times, I even caught myself starting to believe it."

Conn stopped short. His father stopped beside him and stood looking at him.

"Why didn't you tell them the truth?" Rodney Maxwell asked.

The question angered Conn. It was what he had been asking himself.

"Why didn't I just grab a couple of pistols off the table and shoot the lot of them?" he retorted. "It would have killed them quicker and wouldn't have hurt as much."

His father took the cigar from his mouth and inspected the tip of it. "The truth must be pretty bad then. There is no Brain. Is that it, son?"

"There never was one. I'm not saying that only because I know it would be impossible to build such a computer. I'm telling you what the one man in the Galaxy who ought to know told me — the man who commanded the Third Force during the War."

"Foxx Travis! I didn't know he was still alive. You actually talked to him?"

"Yes. He's on Luna, keeping himself alive at low gravity. It took me a couple of years, and I was afraid he'd die before I got to him, but I finally managed to see him."

"What did he tell you?"

"That no such thing as the Brain ever existed." They started walking again, more slowly, toward the far edge of the terrace, with the sky red and orange in front of them.

"The story was all through the Third Force, but it was just one of those wild tales that get started, nobody knows how, among troops. The High Command never denied or even discouraged it. It helped morale, and letting it leak to the enemy was good psychological warfare."

"Klem Zareff says that everybody in the Alliance army heard of the Brain," his father said. "That was why he came here in the first place." He puffed thoughtfully on his cigar. "You said a computer like the Brain would be an impossibility. Why? Wouldn't it be just another computer, only a lot bigger and a lot smarter?"

"Dad, computermen don't like to hear computers called smart," Conn said. "They aren't. The people who build them are smart; a computer only knows what's fed to it. They can hold more information in their banks than a man can in his memory, they can combine it faster, they don't get tired or absent-minded. But they can't imagine, they can't create, and they can't do anything a human brain can't."

"You know, I'd wondered about just that," said his father. "And none of the histories of the War even as much as mentioned the Brain. And I couldn't see why, after the War, they didn't build dozens of them to handle all these Galactic political and economic problems that nobody seems able to solve. A thing like the Brain wouldn't only be useful for war; the people here aren't trying to find it for war purposes."

"You didn't mention any of these doubts to the others, did you?"

"They were just doubts. You knew for sure, and you couldn't tell them."

"I'd come home intending to — tell them there was no Brain, tell them to stop wasting their time hunting for it and start trying to figure out the answers themselves. But I couldn't. They don't believe in the Brain as a tool, to use; it's a machine god that they can bring all their troubles to. You can't take a thing like that away from people without giving them something better."

"I noticed you suggested building a spaceship and agreed with the professor about building a computer. What was your idea? To take their minds off hunting for the Brain and keep them busy?"

Conn shook his head. "I'm serious about the ship — ships. You and Colonel Zareff gave me that idea."

His father looked at him in surprise. "I never said a word in there, and Klem didn't even once mention —"

"Not in Kurt's office; before we went up from the docks. There was Klem, moaning about a good year for melons as though it were a plague, and you selling arms and ammunition by the ton. Why, on Terra or Baldur or Uller, a glass of our brandy brings more than these freighter-captains give us for a cask, and what do you think a colonist on Agramma, or Sekht, or Hachiman, who has to fight for his life against savages and wild animals, would pay for one of those rifles and a thousand rounds of ammunition?"

His father objected. "We can't base the whole economy of a planet on brandy. Only about ten per cent of the arable land on Poictesme will grow wine-melons. And if we start exporting Federation salvage the way you talk of, we'll be selling pieces instead of job lots. We'll net more, but —"

"That's just to get us started. The ships will be used, after that, to get to Tubal-Cain and Hiawatha and the planets of the Beta and Gamma Systems. What I want to see is the mines and factories reopened, people employed, wealth being produced."

"And where'll we sell what we produce? Remember, the mines closed down because there was no more market."

"No more interstellar market, that's true. But there are a hundred and fifty million people on Poictesme.

That's a big enough market and a big enough labor force to exploit the wealth of the Gartner Trisystem. We can have prosperity for everybody on our own resources. Just what do we need that we have to get from outside now?"

His father stopped again and sat down on the edge of a fountain — the same one, possibly, from which Conn had seen dust blowing as the airship had been coming in.

"Conn, that's a dangerous idea. That was what brought on the System States War. The Alliance planets took themselves outside the Federation economic orbit and the Federation crushed them."

Conn swore impatiently. "You've been listening to old Klem Zareff ranting about the Lost Cause and the greedy Terran robber barons holding the Galaxy in economic serfdom while they piled up profits. The Federation didn't fight that war for profits; there weren't any profits to fight for. They fought it because if the System States had won, half of them would be at war among themselves now. Make no mistake about it, politically I'm all for the Federation. But economically, I want to see our people exploiting their own resources for themselves, instead of grieving about lost interstellar trade, and bewailing bumper crops, and searching for a mythical robot god."

"You think, if you can get something like that started, that they'll forget about the Brain?" his father asked skeptically.

"That crowd up in Kurt Fawzi's office? Niflheim, no! They'll go on hunting for the Brain as long as they live, and every day they'll be expecting to find it tomorrow. That'll keep them happy. But they're all old men. The ones I'm interested in are the boys of Charley's age. I'm going to give them too many real things to do — building ships, exploring the rest of the Trisystem, opening mines and factories, producing wealth — for them to get caught in that empty old dream."

He looked down at the dusty fountain on which his father sat. "That ghost-dream haunts this graveyard. I want to give them living dreams that they can make come true."

Conn's father sat in silence for a while, his cigar smoke red in the sunset. "If you can do all that, Conn. . . . You know, I believe you can. I'm with you, as far as I can help, and we'll have a talk with Charley. He's a good boy, Conn, and he has a lot of influence among the other youngsters." He looked at his watch. "We'd better be getting along. You don't want to be late for your own coming-home party."

Rodney Maxwell slid off the edge of the fountain to his feet, hitching at the gunbelt under his coat. Have to dig out his own gun and start wearing it, Conn thought. A man simply didn't go around in public without a gun in Litchfield. It wasn't decent. And he'd be spending a lot of time out in the brush, where he'd really need one.

First thing in the morning, he'd unpack that trunk and go over all those maps. There were half a dozen spaceports and maintenance shops and shipyards within a half-day by airboat, none of which had been looted. He'd look them all over; that would take a couple of weeks. Pick the best shipyard and concentrate on it. Kurt Fawzi'd be the man to recruit labor. Professor Kellton was a scholar, not a scientist. He didn't know beans about hyperdrive engines, but he knew how to do library research.

They came to the edge of High Garden Terrace at the escalator, long motionless, its moving parts rusted fast, that led down to the Mall, and at the bottom of it was Senta's, the tables under the open sky.

A crowd was already gathering. There was Tom Brangwyn, and there was Kurt Fawzi and his wife, and Lynne. And there was Senta herself, fat and dumpy, in one of her preposterous red-and-purple dresses, bustling about, bubbling happily one moment and screaming invective at some laggard waiter the next.

The dinner, Conn knew, would be the best he had eaten in five years, and afterward they would sit in the dim glow of Beta Gartner, sipping coffee and liqueurs, smoking and talking and visiting back and forth from one table to another, as they always did in the evenings at Senta's. Another bit from Eirrarsson's poem came back to him:

> We sit in the twilight, the shadows among,
> And we talk of the happy days when we were brave and
> young.

That was for the old ones, for Colonel Zareff and Judge Ledue and Dolf Kellton, maybe even for Tom Brangwyn and Franz Veltrin and for his father. But his brother Charley and the boys of his generation would have a future to talk about. And so would he, and Lynne Fawzi.

GENESIS

Aboard the ship, there was neither day nor night; the hours slipped gently by, as vistas of star-gemmed blackness slid across the visiscreens. For the crew, time had some meaning — one watch on duty and two off. But for the thousand-odd colonists, the men and women who were to be the spearhead of migration to a new and friendlier planet, it had none. They slept, and played, worked at such tasks as they could invent, and slept again, while the huge ship followed her plotted trajectory.

Kalvar Dard, the army officer who would lead them in their new home, had as little to do as any of his followers. The ship's officers had all the responsibility for the voyage, and, for the first time in over five years, he had none at all. He was finding the unaccustomed idleness more wearying than the hectic work of loading the ship before the blastoff from Doorsha. He went over his landing and security plans again, and found no probable emergency unprepared for. Dard wandered about the ship, talking to groups of his colonists, and found morale even better than he had hoped. He spent hours staring into the forward visiscreens, watching the disc of Tarcesh, the planet of his destination, grow larger and plainer ahead.

Now, with the voyage almost over, he was in the cargo-hold just aft of the Number Seven bulkhead, with six girls to help him, checking construction material which would be needed immediately after landing. The stuff had all been checked two or three times before, but there was no harm in going over it again. It furnished an occupation to fill in the time; it gave Kalvar Dard an excuse for surrounding himself with half a dozen charming girls, and the girls seemed to enjoy being with him. There was tall blonde Olva, the electromagnetician; pert little Varnis, the machinist's helper; Kyna, the surgeon's-aide; dark-haired Analea; Dorita, the accountant; plump little Eldra, the armament technician. At the moment, they were all sitting on or around the desk in the corner of the store-room, going over the inventory when they were not just gabbling.

"Well, how about the rock-drill bitts?" Dorita was asking earnestly, trying to stick to business. "Won't we need them almost as soon as we're off?"

"Yes, we'll have to dig temporary magazines for our explosives, small-arms and artillery ammunition, and storage-pits for our fissionables and radioactives," Kalvar Dard replied. "We'll have to have safe places for that stuff ready before it can be unloaded; and if we run into hard rock near the surface, we'll have to drill holes for blasting-shots."

"The drilling machinery goes into one of those pre-fabricated sheds," Eldra considered. "Will there be room in it for all the bitts, too?"

Kalvar Dard shrugged. "Maybe. If not, we'll cut poles and build racks for them outside. The bitts are nono-steel; they can be stored in the open."

"If there are poles to cut," Olva added.

"I'm not worrying about that," Kalvar Dard replied. "We have a pretty fair idea of conditions on Tareesh; our astronomers have been making telescopic observations for the past fifteen centuries. There's a pretty big Arctic ice-cap, but it's been receding slowly, with a wide belt of what's believed to be open grassland to the south of it, and a belt of what's assumed to be evergreen forest south of that. We plan to land somewhere in the northern hemi-sphere, about the grassland-forest line. And since Tareesh is richer in water that Doorsha, you mustn't think of grassland in terms of our wire-grass plains, or forests in terms of our brush thickets. The vegetation should be much more luxuriant."

"If there's such a large polar ice-cap, the summers ought to be fairly cool, and the winters cold," Varnis reasoned. "I'd think that would mean fur-bearing animals. Colonel, you'll have to shoot me something with a nice soft fur; I like furs."

Kalvar Dard chuckled. "Shoot you nothing, you can shoot your own furs. I've seen your carbine and pistol scores," he began.

There was a sudden suck of air, disturbing the papers on the desk. They all turned to see one of the ship's rocket-boat bays open; a young Air Force lieutenant named Seldar Glav, who would be staying on Tareesh with them to pilot their aircraft, emerged from an open airlock.

"Don't tell me you've been to Tareesh and back in that thing," Olva greeted him.

Seldar Glav grinned at her. "I could have been, at that; we're only twenty or thirty planetary calibers away, now. We ought to be entering Tareeshan atmosphere by the middle of the next watch. I was only checking the boats, to make sure they'll be ready to launch. . . . Colonel Kalvar, would you mind stepping over here? There's something I think you should look at, sir."

Kalvar Dard took one arm from around Analea's waist and lifted the other from Varnis' shoulder, sliding off the desk. He followed Glav into the boat-bay; as they went through the airlock, the cheerfulness left the young lieutenant's face.

"I didn't want to say anything in front of the girls, sir," he began, "but I've been checking boats to make sure we can make a quick getaway. Our meteor-security's gone out. The detectors are deader then the Fourth Dynasty, and the blasters won't synchronize. . . . Did you hear a big thump, about a half an hour ago, Colonel?"

"Yes, I thought the ship's labor-crew was shifting heavy equipment in the hold aft of us. What was it, a meteor-hit?"

"It was. Just aft of Number Ten bulkhead. A meteor about the size of the nose of that rocket-boat."

Kalvar Dard whistled softly. "Great Gods of Power! The detectors must be dead, to pass up anything like that. . . . Why wasn't a boat-stations call sent out?"

"Captain Vlazil was unwilling to risk starting a panic, sir," the Air Force officer replied. "Really, I'm exceeding my orders in mentioning it to you, but I thought you should know. . . ."

Kalvar Dard swore. "It's a blasted pity Captain Vlazil didn't try thinking! Gold-braided quarter-wit! Maybe his crew might panic, but my people wouldn't. . . . I'm going to call the control-room and have it out with him. By the Ten Gods . . . !"

He ran through the airlock and back into the hold, starting toward the intercom-phone beside the desk. Before he could reach it, there was another heavy jar, rocking the entire ship. He, and Seldar Glav, who had followed him out of the boat-bay, and the six girls, who had risen on hearing their commander's angry voice, were all tumbled into a heap. Dard surged to his feet, dragging Kyna up along with him; together, they helped the others to rise. The ship was suddenly filled with jangling bells, and the red danger-lights on the ceiling were flashing on and off.

"Attention! Attention!" the voice of some officer in the control-room blared out of the intercom-speaker. "The ship has just been hit by a large meteor! All compartments between bulkheads Twelve and Thirteen are sealed off. All persons between bulkheads Twelve and Thirteen, put on oxygen helmets and plug in at the nearest phone connection. Your air is leaking, and you can't get out, but if you put on oxygen equipment immediately, you'll be all right. We'll get you out as soon as we can, and in any case, we are only a few hours out of Tareeshan atmosphere. All persons in Compartment Twelve, put on. . . ."

Kalvar Dard was swearing evilly. "That does it! That does it for good! . . . Anybody else in this compartment, below the living quarter level?"

"No, we're the only ones," Analea told him.

"The people above have their own boats; they can look after themselves. You girls, get in that boat, in there. Glav, you and I'll try to warn the people above. . . ."

There was another jar, heavier than the one which had preceded it, throwing them all down again. As they rose, a new voice was shouting over the public-address system:

"*Abandon ship! Abandon ship!* The converters are backfiring, and rocket-fuel is leaking back toward the engine-rooms! An explosion is imminent! Abandon ship, all hands!"

Kalvar Dard and Seldar Glav grabbed the girls and literally threw them through the hatch, into the rocket-boat. Dard pushed Glav in ahead of him, then jumped in. Before he had picked himself up, two or three of the girls were at the hatch, dogging the cover down.

"All right, Glav, blast off!" Dard ordered. "We've got to be at least a hundred miles from this ship when she blows, or we'll blow with her!"

"Don't I know!" Seldar Glav retorted over his shoulder, racing for the controls. "Grab hold of something, everybody; I'm going to fire all jets at once!"

An instant later, while Kalvar Dard and the girls clung to stanchions and pieces of fixed furniture, the boat shot forward out of its housing. When Dard's head had cleared, it was in free flight.

"How was that?" Glav yelled. "Everybody all right?"

He hesitated for a moment. "I think I blacked out for about ten seconds."

Kalvar Dard looked the girls over. Eldra was using a corner of her smock to stanch a nosebleed, and Olva had a bruise over one eye. Otherwise, everybody was in good shape.

"Wonder we didn't all black out, permanently," he said. "Well, put on the visiscreens, and let's see what's going on outside. Olva, get on the radio and try to see if anybody else got away."

"Set course for Tareesh?" Glav asked. "We haven't fuel enough to make it back to Doorsha."

"I was afraid of that," Dard nodded. "Tareesh it is; northern hemisphere, daylight side. Try to get about the edge of the temperate zone, as near water as you can. . . ."

2

They were flung off their feet again, this time backward along the boat. As they picked themselves up, Seldar Glav was shaking his head, sadly. "That was the ship going up," he said; "the blast must have caught us dead astern."

"All right." Kalvar Dard rubbed a bruised forehead. "Set course for Tareesh, then cut out the jets till we're ready to land. And get the screens on, somebody; I want to see what's happened."

The screens glowed; then full vision came on. The planet on which they would land loomed huge before them, its north pole toward them, and its single satellite on the port side. There was no sign of any rocket-boat in either side screen, and the rear-view screen was a blur of yellow flame from the jets.

"Cut the jets, Glav," Dard repeated. "Didn't you hear me?"

"But I did, sir!" Seldar Glav indicated the firing-panel. Then he glanced at the rear-view screen. "The gods help us! It's yellow flame; the jets are burning out!"

Kalvar Dard had not boasted idly when he had said that his people would not panic. All the girls went white, and one or two gave low cries of consternation, but that was all.

"What happens next?" Analea wanted to know. "Do we blow, too?"

"Yes, as soon as the fuel-line burns up to the tanks."

"Can you land on Tareesh before then?" Dard asked.

"I can try. How about the satellite? It's closer."

"It's also airless. Look at it and see for yourself," Kalvar Dard advised. "Not enough mass to hold an atmosphere."

Glav looked at the army officer with new respect. He had always been inclined to think of the Frontier Guards as a gang of scientifically illiterate dirk-and-pistol bravos. He fiddled for a while with instruments on the panel; an automatic computer figured the distance to the planet, the boat's velocity, and the time needed for a landing.

"We have a chance, sir," he said. "I think I can set down in about thirty minutes; that should give us about ten minutes to get clear of the boat, before she blows up."

"All right; get busy, girls," Kalvar Dard said. "Grab everything we'll need. Arms and ammunition first; all of them you can find. After that, warm clothing, bedding, tools and food."

With that, he jerked open one of the lockers and began pulling out weapons. He buckled on a pistol and dagger, and handed other weapon-belts to the girls behind him. He found two of the heavy big-game rifles, and several bandoliers of ammunition for them. He tossed out carbines, and boxes of carbine and pistol cartridges. He found two bomb-bags, each containing six light anti-personnel grenades and a big demolition-bomb. Glancing, now and then, at the forward screen, he caught glimpses of blue sky and green-tinted plains below.

"All right!" the pilot yelled. "We're coming in for a landing! A couple of you stand by to get the hatch open."

There was a jolt, and all sense of movement stopped. A cloud of white smoke drifted past the screens. The girls got the hatch open; snatching up weapons and bedding-wrapped bundles they all scrambled up out of the boat.

There was fire outside. The boat had come down upon a grassy plain; now the grass was burning from the heat of the jets. One by one, they ran forward along the top of the rocket-boat, jumping down to the ground clear of the blaze. Then, with every atom of strength they possessed, they ran away from the doomed boat.

The ground was rough, and the grass high, impeding them. One of the girls tripped and fell; without pausing, two others pulled her to her feet, while another snatched up and slung the carbine she had dropped. Then, ahead, Kalvar Dard saw a deep gully, through which a little stream trickled.

They huddled together at the bottom of it, waiting, for what seemed like a long while. Then a gentle tremor ran through the ground, and swelled to a sickening, heaving shock. A roar of almost palpable sound swept over them, and a flash of blue-white light dimmed the sun above. The sound, the shock, and the searing light did not pass away at once; they continued for seconds that seemed like an eternity. Earth and stones pelted down around them; choking dust rose. Then the thunder and the earth-shock were over; above, incandescent vapors swirled, and darkened into an overhanging pall of smoke and dust.

For a while, they crouched motionless, too stunned to speak. Then shaken nerves steadied and jarred brains cleared. They all rose weakly. Trickles of earth were still coming down from the sides of the gully, and the little stream, which had been clear and sparkling, was roiled with mud. Mechanically, Kalvar Dard brushed the dust from his clothes and looked to his weapons.

"That was just the fuel-tank of a little Class-3 rocket-boat," he said. "I wonder what the explosion of the ship was like." He thought for a moment before continuing. "Glav, I think I know why our jets burned out. We were stern-on to the ship when she blew; the blast drove our flame right back through the jets."

"Do you think the explosion was observed from Doorsha?" Durita inquired, more concerned about the practical aspects of the situation. "The ship, I mean. After all, we have no means of communication, of our own."

"Oh, I shouldn't doubt it; there were observatories all around the planet watching our ship," Kalvar Dard said. "They probably know all about it, by now. But if any of you are thinking about the chances of rescue, forget it. We're stuck here."

"That's right. There isn't another human being within fifty million miles," Seldar Glav said. "And that was the first and only space-ship ever built. It took fifty years to build her, and even allowing twenty for research that wouldn't have to be duplicated, you can figure when we can expect another one."

"The answer to that one is, never. The ship blew up in space; fifty years' effort and fifteen hundred people gone, like that." Kalvar Dard snapped his fingers. "So now, they'll try to keep Doorsha habitable for a few more thousand years by irrigation, and forget about immigrating to Tareesh."

"Well, maybe, in a hundred thousand years, our descendants will build a ship and go to Doorsha, then," Olva considered.

"Our descendants?" Eldra looked at her in surprize. "You mean, then . . . ?"

Kyna chuckled. "Eldra, you are an awful innocent,

about anything that doesn't have a breech-action or a recoil-mechanism," she said. "Why do you think the women on this expedition outnumbered the men seven to five, and why do you think there were so many obstetricians and pediatricians in the med. staff? We were sent out to put a human population on Tareesh, weren't we? Well, here we are."

"But. . . . Aren't we ever going to . . . ?" Varnis began. "Won't we ever see anybody else, or do anything but just live here, like animals, without machines or ground-cars or aircraft or houses or anything?" Then she began to sob bitterly.

Analea, who had been cleaning a carbine that had gotten covered with loose earth during the explosion, laid it down and went to Varnis, putting her arm around the other girl and comforting her. Kalvar Dard picked up the carbine she had laid down.

"Now, let's see," he began. "We have two heavy rifles, six carbines, and eight pistols, and these two bags of bombs. How much ammunition, counting what's in our belts, do we have?"

They took stock of their slender resources, even Varnis joining in the task, as he had hoped she would. There were over two thousand rounds for the pistols, better than fifteen hundred for the carbines, and four hundred for the two big-game guns. They had some spare clothing, mostly space-suit undergarments, enough bed-robes, one hand-axe, two flashlights, a first-aid kit, and three atomic lighters. Each one had a combat-dagger. There was enough tinned food for about a week.

"We'll have to begin looking for game and edible plants, right away," Glav considered. "I suppose there is game, of some sort; but our ammunition won't last forever."

"We'll have to make it last as long as we can; and we'll have to begin improvising weapons," Dard told him.

"Throwing-spears, and throwing-axes. If we can find metal, or any recognizable ore that we can smelt, we'll use that; if not, we'll use chipped stone. Also, we can learn to make snares and traps, after we learn the habits of the animals on this planet. By the time the ammunition's gone, we ought to have learned to do without firearms."

"Think we ought to camp here?"

Kalvar Dard shook his head. "No wood here for fuel, and the blast will have scared away all the game. We'd better go upstream; if we go down, we'll find the water roiled with mud and unfit to drink. And if the game on this planet behave like the game-herds on the wastelands of Doorsha, they'll run for high ground when frightened."

Varnis rose from where she had been sitting. Having mastered her emotions, she was making a deliberate effort to show it.

"Let's make up packs out of this stuff," she suggested. "We can use the bedding and spare clothing to bundle up the food and ammunition."

They made up packs and slung them, then climbed out of the gully. Off to the left, the grass was burning in a wide circle around the crater left by the explosion of the rocket-boat. Kalvar Dard, carrying one of the heavy rifles, took the lead. Beside and a little behind him, Analea walked, her carbine ready. Glav, with the other heavy rifle, brought up in the rear, with Olva covering for him, and between, the other girls walked, two and two.

Ahead, on the far horizon, was a distance-blue line of mountains. The little company turned their faces toward them and moved slowly away, across the empty sea of grass.

3

They had been walking, now, for five years. Kalvar Dard still led, the heavy rifle cradled in the crook of his left arm and a sack of bombs slung from his shoulder, his eyes forever shifting to right and left searching for hidden danger. The clothes in which he had jumped from the rocket-boat were patched and ragged; his shoes had been replaced by high laced buskins of smoke-tanned hide. He was bearded, now, and his hair had been roughly trimmed with the edge of his dagger.

Analea still walked beside him, but her carbine was slung, and she carried three spears with chipped flint heads; one heavy weapon, to be thrown by hand or used for stabbing, and two light javelins to be thrown with the aid of the hooked throwing-stick Glav had invented. Beside her trudged a four-year old boy, hers and Dard's, and on her back, in a fur-lined net bag, she carried their six-month-old baby.

In the rear, Glav still kept his place with the other big-game gun, and Olva walked beside him with carbine and spears; in front of them, their three-year-old daughter toddled. Between vanguard and rearguard, the rest of the party walked: Varnis, carrying her baby on her back, and Dorita, carrying a baby and leading two other children. The baby on her back had cost the life of Kyna in childbirth; one of the others had been left motherless when Eldra had been killed by the Hairy People.

That had been two years ago, in the winter when they had used one of their two demolition-bombs to blast open a cavern in the mountains. It had been a hard winter; two children had died, then — Kyna's firstborn, and the little son of Kalvar Dard and Dorita. It had been their first encounter with the Hairy People, too.

Eldra had gone outside the cave with one of the skin

water-bags, to fill it at the spring. It had been after sunset, but she had carried her pistol, and no one had thought of danger until they heard the two quick shots, and the scream. They had all rushed out, to find four shaggy, manlike things tearing at Eldra with hands and teeth, another lying dead, and a sixth huddled at one side, clutching its abdomen and whimpering. There had been a quick flurry of shots that had felled all four of the assailants, and Seldar Glav had finished the wounded creature with his dagger, but Eldra was dead. They had built a cairn of stones over her body, as they had done over the bodies of the two children killed by the cold. But, after an examination to see what sort of things they were, they had tumbled the bodies of the Hairy People over the cliff. These had been too bestial to bury as befitted human dead, but too manlike to skin and eat as game.

Since then, they had often found traces of the Hairy People, and when they met with them, they killed them without mercy. These were great shambling parodies of humanity, long-armed, short-legged, twice as heavy as men, with close-set reddish eyes and heavy bone-crushing jaws. They may have been incredibly debased humans, or perhaps beasts on the very threshold of man-hood. From what he had seen of conditions on this planet, Kalvar Dard suspected the latter to be the case. In a million or so years, they might evolve into something like humanity. Already, the Hairy ones had learned the use of fire, and of chipped crude stone implements — mostly heavy triangular choppers to be used in the hand, without helves.

Twice, after that night, the Hairy People had attacked them — once while they were on the march, and once in camp. Both assaults had been beaten off without loss to themselves, but at cost of precious ammunition. Once they had caught a band of ten of them swimming a river on logs; they had picked them all off from the bank with their carbines. Once, when Kalvar Dard and Analea had been scouting alone, they had come upon a dozen of them huddled around a fire and had wiped them out with a single grenade. Once, a large band of Hairy People hunted them for two days, but only twice had they come close, and both times, a single shot had sent them all scampering. That had been after the bombing of the group around the fire. Dard was convinced that the beings possessed the rudiments of a language, enough to communicate a few simple ideas, such as the fact that this little tribe of aliens were dangerous in the extreme.

There were Hairy People about now; for the past five days, moving northward through the forest to the open grasslands, the people of Kalvar Dard had found traces of them. Now, as they came out among the seedling growth at the edge of the open plains, everybody was on the alert.

They emerged from the big trees and stopped among the young growth, looking out into the open country. About a mile away, a herd of game was grazing slowly westward. In the distance, they looked like the little horselike things, no higher than a man's waist and heavily maned and bearded, that had been one of their most important sources of meat. For the ten thousandth time, Dard wished, as he strained his eyes, that somebody had thought to secure a pair of binoculars when they had abandoned the rocket-boat. He studied the grazing herd for a long time.

The seedling pines extended almost to the game-herd and would offer concealment for the approach, but the animals were grazing into the wind, and their scent was much keener than their vision. This would prelude one of their favorite hunting techniques, that of lurking in the high grass ahead of the quarry. It had rained heavily in the past few days, and the undermat of dead grass was soaked, making a fire-hunt impossible. Kalvar Dard knew that he could stalk to within easy carbine-shot, but he was unwilling to use cartridges on game; and in view of the proximity of Hairy People, he did not want to divide his band for a drive hunt.

"What's the scheme?" Analea asked him, realizing the problem as well as he did. "Do we try to take them from behind?"

"We'll take them from an angle," he decided. "We'll start from here and work in, closing on them at the rear of the herd. Unless the wind shifts on us, we ought to get within spear-cast. You and I will use the spears; Varnis can come along and cover for us with a carbine. Glav, you and Olva and Dorita stay here with the children and the packs. Keep a sharp lookout; Hairy People around, somewhere." He unslung his rifle and exchanged it for Olva's spears. "We can only eat about two of them before the meat begins to spoil, but kill all you can," he told Analea; "we need the skins."

Then he and the two girls began their slow, cautious, stalk. As long as the grassland was dotted with young trees, they walked upright, making good time, but the last five hundred yards they had to crawl, stopping often to check the wind, while the horse-herd drifted slowly by. Then they were directly behind the herd, with the wind in their faces, and they advanced more rapidly.

"Close enough?" Dard whispered to Analea.

"Yes; I'm taking the one that's lagging a little behind."

"I'm taking the one on the left of it." Kalvar Dard fitted a javelin to the hook of his throwing-stick. "Ready? Now!"

He leaped to his feet, drawing back his right arm and hurling, the throwing-stick giving added velocity to the spear. Beside him, he was conscious of Analea rising and propelling her spear. His missile caught the little bearded pony in the chest; it stumbled and fell forward to its front knees. He snatched another light spear, set it on the hook of the stick and darted it at another horse, which reared, biting at the spear with its teeth. Grabbing the heavy stabbing-spear, he ran forward, finishing it off with a heart-thrust. As he did, Varnis slung her carbine, snatched a stone-headed throwing axe from her belt, and knocked down another horse, then ran forward with her dagger to finish it.

By this time, the herd, alarmed, had stampeded and was galloping away, leaving the dead and dying behind. He and Analea had each killed two; with the one Varnis had knocked down, that made five. Using his dagger, he finished off one that was still kicking on the ground, and then began pulling out the throwing-spears. The girls, shouting in unison, were announcing the successful completion of the hunt; Glav, Olva, and Dorita were coming forward with the children.

It was sunset by the time they had finished the work of skinning and cutting up the horses and had carried the hide-wrapped bundles of meat to the little brook where they had intended camping. There was firewood to be gathered, and the meal to be cooked, and they were all tired.

"We can't do this very often, any more," Kalvar Dard told them, "but we might as well, tonight. Don't bother rubbing sticks for fire; I'll use the lighter."

He got it from a pouch on his belt — a small, gold-plated, atomic lighter, bearing the crest of his old regiment of the Frontier Guards. It was the last one they had, in working order. Piling a handful of dry splinters under the firewood, he held the lighter to it, pressed the activator, and watched the fire eat into the wood.

The greatest achievement of man's civilization, the mastery of the basic, cosmic, power of the atom — being used to kindle a fire of natural fuel, to cook unseasoned meat killed with stone-tipped spears. Dard looked sadly at the twinkling little gadget, then slipped it back into its pouch. Soon it would be worn out, like the other two, and then they would gain fire only by rubbing dry sticks, or hacking sparks from bits of flint or pyrites. Soon, too, the last cartridge would be fired, and then they would perforce depend for protection, as they were already doing for food, upon their spears.

And they were so helpless. Six adults, burdened with seven little children, all of them requiring momently care and watchfulness. If the cartridges could be made to last until they were old enough to fend for themselves. . . . If they could avoid collisions with the Hairy People. . . . Some day, they would be numerous enough for effective mutual protection and support; some day, the ratio of helpless children to able adults would redress itself. Until then, all that they could do would be to survive; day after day, they must follow the game-herds.

4

For twenty years, now, they had been following the game. Winters had come, with driving snow, forcing horses and deer into the woods, and the little band of humans to the protection of mountain caves. Springtime followed, with fresh grass on the plains and plenty of meat for the people of Kalvar Dard. Autumns followed summers, with fire-hunts, and the smoking and curing of meat and hides. Winters followed autumns, and springtimes came again, and thus until the twentieth year after the landing of the rocket-boat.

Kalvar Dard still walked in the lead, his hair and beard flecked with gray, but he no longer carried the heavy rifle; the last cartridge for that had been fired long ago. He carried the hand-axe, fitted with a long helve, and a spear with a steel head that had been worked painfully from the receiver of a useless carbine. He still had his pistol, with eight cartridges in the magazine, and his dagger, and the bomb-bag, containing the big demolition-bomb and one grenade. The last shred of clothing from the ship was gone, now; he was clad in a sleeveless tunic of skin and horsehide buskins.

Analea no longer walked beside him; eight years before, she had broken her back in a fall. It had been impossible to move her, and she stabbed herself with her dagger to save a cartridge. Seldar Glav had broken through the ice while crossing a river, and had lost his rifle; the next day he died of the chill he had taken. Olva had been killed by the Hairy People, the night they had attacked the camp, when Varnis' child had been killed.

They had beaten off that attack, shot or speared ten of the huge sub-men, and the next morning they buried their dead after their custom, under cairns of stone. Varnis had watched the burial of her child with blank, uncomprehending eyes, then she had turned to Kalvar Dard and said something that had horrified him more than any wild outburst of grief could have.

"Come on, Dard; what are we doing this for? You promised you'd take us to Tareesh, where we'd have good houses, and machines, and all sorts of lovely things to eat and wear. I don't like this place, Dard; I want to go to Tareesh."

From that day on, she had wandered in merciful darkness. She had not been idiotic, or raving mad; she had just escaped from a reality that she could no longer bear.

Varnis, lost in her dream-world, and Dorita, hard-faced and haggard, were the only ones left, beside Kalvar Dard, of the original eight. But the band had grown, meanwhile, to more than fifteen. In the rear, in Seldar Glav's old place, the son of Kalvar Dard and Analea walked. Like his father, he wore a pistol, for which he had six rounds, and a dagger, and in his hand he carried a stone-headed killing-maul with a three-foot handle which he had made for himself. The woman who walked beside him and carried his spears was the daughter of Glav and Olva; in a net-bag on her back she carried their infant child. The first Tareeshan born of Tareeshan parents; Kalvar Dard often looked at his little grandchild during nights in camp and days on the trail, seeing, in that tiny fur-swaddled morsel of humanity, the meaning and purpose of all that he did. Of the older girls, one or two were already pregnant, now; this tiny threatened beachhead of humanity was expanding, gaining strength. Long after man had died out on Doorsha and the dying planet itself had become an arid waste, the progeny of this little band would continue to grow and to dominate the younger planet, nearer the sun. Some day, an even mightier civilization than the one he had left would rise here. . . .

All day the trail had wound upward into the mountains. Great cliffs loomed above them, and little streams spumed and dashed in rocky gorges below. All day, the Hairy People had followed, fearful to approach too close, unwilling to allow their enemies to escape. It had started when they had rushed the camp, at daybreak; they had been beaten off, at cost of almost all the ammunition, and the death of one child. No sooner had the tribe of Kalvar Dard taken the trail, however, than they had been pressing after them. Dard had determined to cross the mountains, and had led his people up a game-trail, leading toward the notch of a pass high against the skyline.

The shaggy ape-things seemed to have divined his purpose. Once or twice, he had seen hairy brown shapes dodging among the rocks and stunted trees to the left. They were trying to reach the pass ahead of him. Well, if they did. . . . He made a quick mental survey of his resources. His pistol, and his son's, and Dorita's, with eight, and six, and seven rounds. One grenade, and the big demolition bomb, too powerful to be thrown by hand, but which could be set for delayed explosion and dropped over a cliff or left behind to explode among pursuers. Five steel daggers, and plenty of spears and slings and axes. Himself, his son and his son's woman, Dorita, and four or five of the older boys and girls, who would make effective front-line fighters. And Varnis, who might come out of her private dream-world long enough to give account for herself, and even the tiniest of the walking children could throw stones or light spears. Yes, they could force the pass, if the Hairy People reached it ahead of them, and then seal it shut with the heavy bomb. What lay on the other side, he did not know; he wondered how much game there would be, and if there were Hairy People on that side, too.

Two shots slammed quickly behind him. He dropped his axe and took a two-hand grip on his stabbing-spear as he turned. His son was hurrying forward, his pistol drawn, glancing behind as he came.

"Hairy People. Four," he reported. "I shot two; she threw a spear and killed another. The other ran."

The daughter of Seldar Glav and Olva nodded in agreement.

"I had no time to throw again," she said, "and Bo-Bo would not shoot the one that ran."

Kalvar Dard's son, who had no other name than the one his mother had called him as a child, defended himself. "He was running away. It is the rule: *use bullets only to save life, where a spear will not serve.*"

Kalvar Dard nodded. "You did right, son," he said, taking out his own pistol and removing the magazine, from which he extracted two cartridges. "Load these into your pistol; four rounds aren't enough. Now we each have six. Go back to the rear, keep the little ones moving, and don't let Varnis get behind."

"That is right. *We must all look out for Varnis, and take care of her,*" the boy recited obediently. "That is the rule."

He dropped to the rear. Kalvar Dard holstered his pistol and picked up his axe, and the column moved forward again. They were following a ledge, now; on the left, there was a sheer drop of several hundred feet, and on the right a cliff rose above them, growing higher and steeper as the trail slanted upward. Dard was worried about the ledge; if it came to an end, they would all be trapped. No one would escape. He suddenly felt old and unutterably weary. It was a frightful weight that he bore — responsibility for an entire race.

Suddenly, behind him, Dorita fired her pistol upward. Dard sprang forward — there was no room for him to jump aside — and drew his pistol. The boy, Bo-Bo, was trying to find a target from his position in the rear. Then Dard saw the two Hairy People; the boy fired, and the stone fell, all at once.

It was a heavy stone, half as big as a man's torso, and it almost missed Kalvar Dard. If it had hit him directly, it would have killed him instantly, mashing him to a bloody pulp; as it was, he was knocked flat, the stone pinning his legs.

At Bo-Bo's shot, a hairy body plummeted down to hit the ledge. Bo-Bo's woman instantly ran it through with one of her spears. The other ape-thing, the one Dorita had shot, was still clinging to a rock above. Two of the children scampered up to it and speared it repeatedly, screaming like little furies. Dorita and one of the older girls got the rock off Kalvar Dard's legs and tried to help him to his feet, but he collapsed, unable to stand. Both his legs were broken.

This was it, he thought, sinking back.

"Dorita, I want you to run ahead and see what the

trail's like," he said. "See if the ledge is passable. And find a place, not too far ahead, where we can block the trail by exploding that demolition-bomb. It has to be close enough for a couple of you to carry or drag me and get me there in one piece."

"What are you going to do?"

"What do you think?" he retorted. "I have both legs broken. You can't carry me with you; if you try it, they'll catch us and kill us all. I'll have to stay behind; I'll block the trail behind you, and get as many of them as I can while I'm at it. Now, run along and do as I said."

She nodded. "I'll be back as soon as I can," she agreed.

The others were crowding around Dard. Bo-Bo bent over him, perplexed and worried. "What are you going to do, father?" he asked. "You are hurt. Are you going to go away and leave us, as mother did when she was hurt?"

"Yes, son; I'll have to. You carry me on ahead a little, when Dorita gets back, and leave me where she shows you to. I'm going to stay behind and block the trail, and kill a few Hairy People. I'll use the big bomb."

"The *big* bomb? The one nobody dares throw?" The boy looked at his father in wonder.

"That's right. Now, when you leave me, take the others and get away as fast as you can. Don't stop till you're up to the pass. Take my pistol and dagger, and the axe and the big spear, and take the little bomb, too. Take everything I have, only leave the big bomb with me. I'll need that."

Dorita rejoined them. "There's a waterfall ahead. We can get around it, and up to the pass. The way's clear and easy; if you put off the bomb just this side of it, you'll start a rock-slide that'll block everything."

"All right. Pick me up, a couple of you. Don't take hold of me below the knees. And hurry."

✱　　✱　　✱

A hairy shape appeared on the ledge below them; one of the older boys used his throwing-stick to drive a javelin into it. Two of the girls picked up Dard; Bo-Bo and his woman gathered up the big spear and the axe and the bomb-bag.

They hurried forward, picking their way along the top of a talus of rubble at the foot of the cliff, and came to where the stream gushed out of a narrow gorge. The air was wet with spray there, and loud with the roar of the waterfall. Kalvar Dard looked around; Dorita had chosen the spot well. Not even a sure-footed mountain-goat could make the ascent, once that gorge was blocked.

"All right; put me down here," he directed. "Bo-Bo, take my belt, and give me the big bomb. You have one light grenade; know how to use it?"

"Of course, you have often showed me. I turn the top, and then press in the little thing on the side, and hold it in till I throw. I throw it at least a spear-cast, and drop to the ground or behind something."

"That's right. And use it only in greatest danger, to save everybody. Spare your cartridges; use them only to save life. And save everything of metal, no matter how small."

"Yes. Those are the rules. I will follow them, and so will the others. And we will always take care of Varnis."

"Well, goodbye, son." He gripped the boy's hand. "Now get everybody out of here; don't stop till you're at the pass."

"You're not staying behind!" Varnis cried. "Dard, you promised us! I remember, when we were all in the ship together — you and I and Analea and Olva and Dorita and Eldra and, oh, what was that other girl's name, Kyna! And we were all having such a nice time, and you were telling us how we'd all come to Tareesh, and we were having such fun talking about it. . . ."

"That's right, Varnis," he agreed. "And so I will. I have something to do, here, but I'll meet you on top of the mountain, after I'm through, and in the morning we'll all go to Tareesh."

She smiled — the gentle, childlike smile of the harmlessly mad — and turned away. The son of Kalvar Dard made sure that she and all the children were on the way, and then he, too, turned and followed them, leaving Dard alone.

Alone, with a bomb and a task. He'd borne that task for twenty years, now; in a few minutes, it would be ended, with an instant's searing heat. He tried not to be too glad; there were so many things he might have done, if he had tried harder. Metals, for instance. Somewhere there surely must be ores which they could have smelted, but he had never found them. And he might have tried catching some of the little horses they hunted for food, to break and train to bear burdens. And the alphabet — why hadn't he taught it to Bo-Bo and the daughter of Seldar Glav, and laid on them an obligation to teach the others? And the grass-seeds they used for making flour sometimes; they should have planted fields of the better kinds, and patches of edible roots, and returned at the proper time to harvest them. There were so many things, things that none of those young savages or their children would think of in ten thousand years. . . .

Something was moving among the rocks, a hundred yards away. He straightened, as much as his broken legs would permit, and watched. Yes, there was one of them, and there was another, and another. One rose from behind a rock and came forward at a shambling run, making bestial sounds. Then two more lumbered into sight, and in a moment the ravine was alive with them. They were almost upon him when Kalvar Dard pressed in the thumbpiece of the bomb; they were clutching at him when he released it. He felt a slight jar. . . .

*　　*　　*

When they reached the pass, they all stopped as the son of Kalvar Dard turned and looked back. Dorita stood beside him, looking toward the waterfall too; she also knew what was about to happen. The others merely gaped in blank incomprehension, or grasped their weapons, thinking that the enemy was pressing close behind and that they were making a stand here. A few of the smaller boys and girls began picking up stones.

Then a tiny pin-point of brilliance winked, just below where the snow-fed stream vanished into the gorge. That was all, for an instant, and then a great fire-shot cloud swirled upward, hundreds of feet into the air; there was a crash, louder than any sound any of them except Dorita and Varnis had ever heard before.

"He did it!" Dorita said softly.

"Yes, he did it. My father was a brave man," Bo-Bo replied. "We are safe, now."

Varnis, shocked by the explosion, turned and stared at him, and then she laughed happily. "Why, there you are, Dard!" she exclaimed. "I was wondering where you'd gone. What did you do after we left?"

"What do you mean?" The boy was puzzled, not knowing how much he looked like his father, when his father had been an officer of the Frontier Guards, twenty years before.

His puzzlement worried Varnis vaguely. "You.... You are Dard, aren't you?" she asked. "But that's silly; of course you're Dard! Who else could you be?"

"Yes. I am Dard," the boy said, remembering that it was the rule for everybody to be kind to Varnis and to pretend to agree with her. Then another thought struck him. His shoulders straightened. "Yes. I am Dard, son of Dard," he told them all. "I lead, now. Does anybody say no?"

He shifted his axe and spear to his left hand and laid

his right hand on the butt of his pistol, looking sternly at Dorita. If any of them tried to dispute his claim, it would be she. But instead, she gave him the nearest thing to a real smile that had crossed her face in years.

"You are Dard," she told him; "you lead us, now."

"But of course Dard leads! Hasn't he always led us?" Varnis wanted to know. "Then what's all the argument about? And tomorrow he's going to take us to Tareesh, and we'll have houses and ground-cars and aircraft and gardens and lights, and all the lovely things we want. Aren't you, Dard?"

"Yes, Varnis; I will take you all to Tareesh, to all the wonderful things," Dard, son of Dard, promised, for such was the rule about Varnis.

Then he looked down from the pass into the country beyond. There were lower mountains, below, and foot-hills, and a wide blue valley, and, beyond that, distant peaks reared jaggedly against the sky. He pointed with his father's axe.

"We go down that way," he said.

So they went, down, and on, and on, and on. The last cartridge was fired; the last sliver of Doorshan metal wore out or rusted away. By then, however, they had learned to make chipped stone, and bone, and reindeer-horn serve their needs. Century after century, millennium after millennium, they followed the game-herds from birth to death, and birth replenished their numbers faster than death depleted. Bands grew in numbers and split; young men rebelled against the rule of the old and took their women and children elsewhere.

They hunted down the hairy Neanderthalers, and exterminated them ruthlessly, the origin of their implacable hatred lost in legend. All that they remembered, in the misty, confused, way that one remembers a dream, was that there had once been a time of happiness and plenty, and that there was a goal to which they would some day attain. They left the mountains — were they the Caucasus? The Alps? The Pamirs? — and spread outward, conquering as they went.

We find their bones, and their stone weapons, and their crude paintings, in the caves of Cro-Magnon and Grimaldi and Altimira and Mas-d'Azil; the deep layers of horse and reindeer and mammoth bones at their feasting-place at Solutre. We wonder how and whence a race so like our own came into a world of brutish sub-humans.

Just as we wonder, too, at the network of canals which radiate from the polar caps of our sister planet, and speculate on the possibility that they were the work of hands like our own. And we concoct elaborate jokes about the "Men From Mars" — *ourselves*.

OPERATION R.S.V.P

Vladmir N. Dzhoubinsky, Foreign Minister, Union of East European Soviet Republics, to Wu Fung Tung, Foreign Minister, United Peoples' Republics of East Asia:

15 Jan. 1984
Honored Sir:

Pursuant to our well known policy of exchanging military and scientific information with the Government, of friendly Powers, my Government takes great pleasure in announcing the completely successful final tests of our new nuclear-rocket guided missile Marxist Victory. The test launching was made from a position south of Lake Balkash; the target was located in the East Siberian Sea.

In order to assist you in appreciating the range of the new guided missile Marxist Victory, let me point out that the distance from launching-site to target is somewhat over 50 percent greater than the distance from launching-site to your capital, Nanking.

My Government is still hopeful that your Government will revise its present intransigeant position on the Khakum River dispute.

I have the honor, etc., etc., etc.,

V. N. Dzhoubinsky

*   *   *

Wu Fung Tung, to Vladmir N. Dzhoubinsky:

7 Feb., 1984

Estimable Sir:

My Government was most delighted to learn of the splendid triumph of your Government in developing the new guided missile Marxist Victory, and at the same time deeply relieved. We had, of course, detected the release of nuclear energy incident to the test, and inasmuch as it had obviously originated in the disintegration of a quantity of Uranium 235, we had feared that an explosion had occurred at your Government's secret uranium plant at Khatanga. We have long known of the lax security measures in effect at this plant, and have, as a consequence, been expecting some disaster there.

I am therefore sure that your Government will be equally gratified to learn of the perfection, by my Government, of our own new guided missile Celestial Destroyer, which embodies, in greatly improved form, many of the features of your own Government's guided missile Marxist Victory. Naturally, your own scientific warfare specialists have detected the release of energy incident to the explosion of our own improved thorium-hafnium interaction bomb; this bomb was exploded over the North Polar ice cap, about two hundred miles south of the Pole, on about 35 degrees East Longitude, almost due north of your capital city of Moscow. The launching was made from a site in Thibet.

Naturally, my Government cannot deviate from our present just and reasonable attitude in the Khakum River question. Trusting that your Government will realize this, I have the honor to be,

Your obedient and respectful servant,

Wu Fung Tung

*   *   *

From *N. Y. Times*, Feb. 20, 1984:

AFGHAN RULER FÊTED AT NANKING
Ameer Shere Ali Abdallah Confers
with
UPREA Pres. Sung Li-Yin

UEESR Foreign Minister Dzhoubinsky to Maxim G. Krylenkoff, Ambassador at Nanking:

3 March, 1984
Comrade Ambassador:
It is desired that you make immediate secret and confidential repeat secret and confidential inquiry as to the whereabouts of Dr. Dimitri O. Voronoff, the noted Soviet rocket expert, designer of the new guided missile Marxist Victory, who vanished a week ago from the Josef Vissarionovitch Djugashvli Reaction-Propulsion Laboratories at Molotovgorod. It is feared in Government circles that this noted scientist has been abducted by agents of the United Peoples' Republics of East Asia, possibly to extract from him, under torture, information of a secret technical nature.

As you know, this is but the latest of a series of such disappearances, beginning about five years ago, when the Khakum River question first arose.

Your utmost activity in this matter is required.

Dzhoubinsky

*　　*　　*

Ambassador Krylenkoff to Foreign Minister Dzhoubinsky:

9 March, 1984
Comrade Foreign Minister:
Since receipt of yours of 3/3/'84, I have been utilizing

all resources at my disposal in the matter of the noted scientist D. O. Voronoff, and availing myself of all sources of information, e.g., spies, secret agents, disaffected elements of the local population, and including two UPREA Cabinet Ministers on my payroll. I regret to report that results of this investigation have been entirely negative. No one here appears to know anything of the whereabouts of Dr. Voronoff.

At the same time, there is considerable concern in UPREA Government circles over the disappearances of certain prominent East Asian scientists, e.g., Dr. Hong Foo, the nuclear physicist; Dr. Hin Yang-Woo, the great theoretical mathematician; Dr. Mong Shing, the electronics expert. I am informed that UPREA Government sources are attributing these disappearances to us.

I can only say that I am sincerely sorry that this is not the case.

Krylenkoff

*   *   *

Wu Fung Tung to Vladmir N. Dzhoubinsky:

21 April, 1984
Estimable Sir:

In accordance with our established policy of free exchange with friendly Powers of scientific information, permit me to inform your Government that a new mutated disease-virus has been developed in our biological laboratories, causing a highly contagious disease similar in symptoms to bubonic plague, but responding to none of the treatments for this latter disease. This new virus strain was accidentally produced in the course of some experiments with radioactivity.

In spite of the greatest care, it is feared that this virus has spread beyond the laboratory in which it was developed. We warn you most urgently of the danger that it may have spread to the UEESR; enclosed are a list of symptoms, etc.

My Government instructs me to advise your Government that the attitude of your Government in the Khakum River question is utterly unacceptable, and will require considerable revision before my Government can even consider negotiation with your Government on the subject. Your obedient and respectful servant,

Wu Fung Tung

*   *   *

From *N. Y. Times*, May 12, 1984:

AFGHAN RULER FÊTED AT MOSCOW
Ameer sees Red Square Troop Review;
Confers with Premier-President Mouzorgin

*   *   *

Sing Yat, UPREA Ambassador at Moscow, to Wu Fung Tung:

26 June, 1984
Venerable and Honored Sir:

I regret humbly that I can learn nothing whatever about the fate of the learned scholars of science of whom you inquire, namely: Hong Foo, Hin Yang-Woo, Mong Shing, Yee Ho Li, Wong Fat, and Bao Hu-Shin. This inability may be in part due to incompetence of my unworthy self, but none of my many sources of information, including Soviet Minister of Police Morgodoff, who is on my payroll, can furnish any useful data whatever. I am informed, however, that the UEESR Government is deeply concerned about similar disappearances of some of the foremost of their own scientists, including Voronoff, Jirnikov, Kagorinoff, Bakhorin, Himmelfarber and Pavlovinsky, all of whose dossiers are on file with our

Bureau of Foreign Intelligence. I am further informed that the Government of the UEESR ascribes these disappearances to our own activities.

Ah, Venerable and Honored Sir, if this were only true!

Kindly condescend to accept compliments of,

　　Sing Yat

　　　　*　　　　*　　　　*

Dzhoubinsky to Wu Fung Tung:

6 October, 1984

Honored Sir:

Pursuant to our well known policy of exchanging scientific information with the Governments of friendly Powers, my Government takes the greatest pleasure in announcing a scientific discovery of inestimable value to the entire world. I refer to nothing less than a positive technique for liquidating rats as a species.

This technique involves treatment of male rats with certain types of hard radiations, which not only renders them reproductively sterile but leaves the rodents so treated in full possession of all other sexual functions and impulses. Furthermore, this condition of sterility is venereally contagious, so that one male rat so treated will sterilize all female rats with which it comes in contact, and these, in turn, will sterilize all male rats coming in contact with them. Our mathematicians estimate that under even moderately favorable circumstances, the entire rat population of the world could be sterilized from one male rat in approximately two hundred years.

Rats so treated have already been liberated in the granaries at Odessa; in three months, rat-trappings there have fallen by 26.4 percent, and grain-losses to rats by 32.09 percent.

We are shipping you six dozen sterilized male rats, which you can use for sterilization stock, and, by so augmenting their numbers, may duplicate our own successes.

Curiously enough, this effect of venereally contagious sterility was discovered quite accidentally, in connection with the use of hard radiations for human sterilization (criminals, mental defectives, etc.). Knowing the disastrous possible effects of an epidemic of contagious human sterility, all persons so sterilized were liquidated as soon as the contagious nature of their sterility had been discovered, with the exception of a dozen or so convicts, who had been released before this discovery was made. It is believed that at least some of them have made their way over the border and into the territory of the United Peoples' Republics of East Asia. I must caution your Government to be on the lookout of them. Among a people still practicing ancestor-worship, an epidemic of sterility would be a disaster indeed.

My Government must insist that your Government take some definite step toward the solution of the Khakum River question; the present position of the Government of the United Peoples' Republics of East Asia on this subject is utterly unacceptable to the Government of the Union of East European Soviet Republics, and must be revised very considerably.

I have the honor, etc., etc.,
Vladmir N. Dzhoubinsky

*　　　*　　　*

Coded radiogram, Dzhoubinsky to Krylenkoff:

25 OCTOBER, 1984
ASCERTAIN IMMEDIATELY CAUSE OF RELEASE OF NUCLEAR ENERGY VICINITY OF NOVA ZEMBLA THIS AM
DZHOUBINSKY

*   *   *

Coded radiogram, Wu Fung Tung to Sing Yat:

25 OCTOBER, 1984
ASCERTAIN IMMEDIATELY CAUSE OF RE-
LEASE OF NUCLEAR ENERGY VICINITY OF NOVA
ZEMBLA THIS AM
WU

*   *   *

Letter from the Ameer of Afghanistan to UEESR Premier-President Mouzorgin and UPREA President Sung
Li-Yin:

26 October, 1984
SHERE ALI ABDALLAH, Ameer of Afghanistan,
Master of Kabul, Lord of Herat and Kandahar, Keeper of
Khyber Pass, Defender of the True Faith, Servant of the
Most High and Sword-Hand of the Prophet; Ph.D.
(Princeton); Sc.B. (Massachusetts Institute of Techno-
logy); M.A. (Oxford): to their Excellencies A.A. Mou-
zorgin, Premier-President of the Union of East European
Soviet Republics, and Sung Li-Yin, President of the
United Peoples' Republics of East Asia,
Greetings, in the name of Allah!
For the past five years, I have watched, with growing
concern, the increasing tensions between your Excellencies' respective Governments, allegedly arising out of the
so-called Khakum River question. It is my conviction that
this Khakum River dispute is the utterly fraudulent device
by which both Governments hope to create a pretext for
the invasion of India, each ostensibly to rescue that un-
happy country from the rapacity of the other. Your Excellencies must surely realize that this is a contingency
which the Government of the Kingdom of Afghanistan
cannot and will not permit; it would mean nothing short

of the national extinction of the Kingdom of Afghanistan, and the enslavement of the Afghan people.

Your Excellencies will recall that I discussed this matter most urgently on the occasions of my visits to your respective capitals of Moscow and Nanking, and your respective attitudes, on those occasions, has firmly convinced me that neither of your Excellencies is by nature capable of adopting a rational or civilized attitude toward this question. It appears that neither of your Excellencies has any intention of abandoning your present war of mutual threats and blackmail until forced to do so by some overt act on the part of one or the other of your Excellencies' Governments, which would result in physical war of pan-Asiatic scope and magnitude. I am further convinced that this deplorable situation arises out of the megalomaniac ambitions of the Federal Governments of the UEESR and the UPREA, respectively, and that the different peoples of what you unblushingly call your "autonomous" republics have no ambitions except, on a rapidly diminishing order of probability, to live out their natural span of years in peace. Therefore:

In the name of ALLAH, the Merciful, the Compassionate: We, Shere Ali Abdallah, Ameer of Afghanistan, etc., do decree and command that the political entities known as the Union of East European Soviet Republics and the United Peoples' Republics of East Asia respectively are herewith abolished and dissolved into their constituent autonomous republics, each one of which shall hereafter enjoy complete sovereignty within its own borders as is right and proper.

Now, in case either of you gentlemen feel inclined to laugh this off, let me remind you of the series of mysterious disappearances of some of the most noted scientists of both the UEESR and the UPREA, and let me advise your Excellencies that these scientists are now residents and subjects of the Kingdom of Afghanistan, and are here engaged in research and development work for my Government. These gentlemen were not abducted, as you gentlemen seem to believe; they came here of their own free will, and ask nothing better than to remain here, where they are treated with dignity and honor, given material rewards—riches, palaces, harems, retinues of servants, etc.—and are also free from the intellectual and ideological restraints which make life so intolerable in your respective countries to any man above the order of intelligence of a cretin. In return for these benefactions, these eminent scientists have developed, for my Government, certain weapons. For example:

1.) A nuclear-rocket guided missile, officially designated as the Sword of Islam, vastly superior to your Excellencies' respective guided missiles Marxist Victory and Celestial Destroyer. It should be; it was the product of the joint efforts of Dr. Voronoff and Dr. Bao Hu-Shin, whom your Excellencies know.

2.) A new type of radar-radio-electronic defense screen, which can not only detect the approach of a guided missile, at any velocity whatever, but will automatically capture and redirect same. In case either of your Excellencies doubt this statement, you are invited to aim a rocket at some target in Afghanistan and see what happens.

3.) Both the UPREA mutated virus and the UEESR contagious sterility, with positive vaccines against the former and means of instrumental detection of the latter.

4.) A technique for initiating and controlling the Bethe carbon-hydrogen cycle. We are now using this as a source of heat for industrial and even domestic purposes, and we also have a carbon-hydrogen cycle bomb. Such a bomb, delivered by one of our Sword of Islam Mark IV's, was activated yesterday over the Northern tip of Nova Zembla, at an altitude of four miles. I am enclosing photographic reproductions of views of this test, televised to Kabul by an accompanying Sword of Islam Mark V observation rocket. I am informed that expeditions have been sent by both the UEESR and the UPREA to investigate; they should find some very interesting conditions. For one thing, they won't need their climbing equipment to get over the Nova Zembla Glacier; the Nova Zembla Glacier isn't there, any more.

5.) A lithium bomb. This has not been tested, yet. A lithium bomb is nothing for a country the size of Afghanistan to let off inside its own borders. We intend making a test with it within the next ten days, however If your Excellencies will designate a target, which must be at the center of an uninhabited area at least five hundred miles square, the test can be made in perfect safety. If not, I cannot answer the results; that will be in the hands of Allah, Who has ordained all things. No doubt Allah has ordained the destruction of either Moscow or Nanking; whichever city Allah has elected to erase, I will make it my personal responsibility to see to it that the other isn't slighted, either.

However, if your Excellencies decide to accede to my modest and reasonable demands, not later than one week from today, this test-launching will be cancelled as unnecessary. Of course, that would leave unsettled a bet I have made with Dr. Hong Foo—a star sapphire against his favorite Persian concubine—that the explosion of a lithium bomb will not initiate a chain reaction in the Earth's crust and so disintegrate this planet. This, of course, is a minor consideration, unworthy of Your notice.

Of course, I am aware that both your Excellencies have, in the past, fomented mutual jealousies and suspicions among the several "autonomous" republics under your respective jurisdictions, as an instrument of policy. If these peoples were, at this time, to receive full independence, the present inevitability of a pan-Asiatic war on a grand scale would be replaced only by the inevitability of a pan-Asiatic war by detail. Obviously, some single supra-national sovereignty is needed to maintain peace, and such a sovereignty should be established under some leadership not hitherto associated with either the former UEESR or the former UPREA. I humbly offer myself as President of such a supra-national organization, counting as a matter of course upon the whole-hearted support and co-operation of both your Excellencies. It might be well if both your Excellencies were to come here to Kabul to confer with me on this subject at your very earliest convenience.

The Peace of Allah be upon both your Excellencies!
Shere Ali Abdallah, Ph.D., Sc.B., M.A.

※   ※   ※

From *N. Y. Times*, Oct. 30, 1984:
MOUZORGIN, SUN LI-YIN,
FÊTED AT KABUL
Confer With Ameer;
Discuss Peace Plans
Surprise Developments Seen. . . .

THE ANSWER

For a moment, after the screen door snapped and wakened him, Lee Richardson sat breathless and motionless, his eyes still closed, trying desperately to cling to the dream and print it upon his conscious memory before it faded.

"Are you there, Lee?" he heard Alexis Pitov's voice.

"Yes, I'm here. What time is it?" he asked, and then added, "I fell asleep. I was dreaming."

It was all right; he was going to be able to remember. He could still see the slim woman with the graying blonde hair, playing with the little dachshund among the new-fallen leaves on the lawn. He was glad they'd both been in this dream together; these dream-glimpses were all he'd had for the last fifteen years, and they were too precious to lose. He opened his eyes. The Russian was sitting just outside the light from the open door of the bungalow, lighting a cigarette. For a moment, he could see the blocky, high-cheeked face, now pouched and wrinkled, and then the flame went out and there was only the red coal glowing in the darkness. He closed his eyes again, and the dream picture came back to him, the woman catching the little dog and raising her head as though to speak to him.

"Plenty of time, yet." Pitov was speaking German instead of Spanish, as they always did between themselves. "They're still counting down from minus three hours. I just phoned the launching site for a jeep. Eugenio's been there ever since dinner; they say he's running around like a cat looking for a place to have her first litter of kittens."

He chuckled. This would be something new for Eugenio Galvez — for which he could be thankful.

"I hope the generators don't develop any last-second bugs," he said. "We'll only be a mile and a half away, and that'll be too close to fifty kilos of negamatter if the field collapses."

"It'll be all right," Pitov assured him. "The bugs have all been chased out years ago."

"Not out of those generators in the rocket. They're new." He fumbled in his coat pocket for his pipe and tobacco. "I never thought I'd run another nuclear-bomb test, as long as I lived."

"Lee!" Pitov was shocked. "You mustn't call it that. It isn't that, at all. It's purely a scientific experiment."

"Wasn't that all any of them were? We made lots of experiments like this, back before 1969." The memories of all those other tests, each ending in an Everest-high mushroom column, rose in his mind. And the end result — the United States and the Soviet Union blasted to rubble, a whole hemisphere pushed back into the Dark Ages, a quarter of a billion dead. Including a slim woman with graying blonde hair, and a little red dog, and a girl from Odessa whom Alexis Pitov had been going to marry. "Forgive me, Alexis. I just couldn't help remembering. I suppose it's this shot we're going to make, tonight. It's so much like the other ones, before —" He hesitated slightly. "Before the Auburn Bomb."

There; he'd come out and said it. In all the years they'd worked together at the *Instituto Argentino de Ciencia Fisica*, that had been unmentioned between them. The families of hanged cutthroats avoid mention of ropes and knives. He thumbed the old-fashioned American lighter and held it to his pipe. Across the veranda, in the darkness, he knew that Pitov was looking intently at him.

"You've been thinking about that, lately, haven't you?" the Russian asked, and then, timidly: "Was that what you were dreaming of?"

"Oh, no, thank heaven!"

"I think about it, too, always. I suppose —" He seemed relieved, now that it had been brought out into the open and could be discussed. "You saw it fall, didn't you?"

"That's right. From about thirty miles away. A little closer than we'll be to this shot, tonight. I was in charge of the investigation at Auburn, until we had New York and Washington and Detroit and Mobile and San Francisco to worry about. Then what had happened to Auburn wasn't important, any more. We were trying to get evidence to lay before the United Nations. We kept at it for about twelve hours after the United Nations had ceased to exist."

"I could never understand about that, Lee. I don't know what the truth is; I probably never shall. But I know that my government did not launch that missile. During the first days after yours began coming in, I talked to people who had been in the Kremlin at the time. One had been in the presence of Klyzenko himself when the news of your bombardment arrived. He said that Klyzenko was absolutely stunned. We always believed that your government decided upon a preventive surprise attack, and picked out a town, Auburn, New York, that had been hit by one of our first retaliation missiles, and claimed that it had been hit first."

He shook his head. "Auburn was hit an hour before the first American missile was launched. I know that to be a fact. We could never understand why you launched just that one, and no more until after ours began landing on you; why you threw away the advantage of surprise and priority of attack —"

"Because we didn't do it, Lee!" The Russian's voice trembled with earnestness. "You believe me when I tell you that?"

"Yes, I believe you. After all that happened, and all that you, and I, and the people you worked with, and the people I worked with, and your government, and mine, have been guilty of, it would be a waste of breath for either of us to try to lie to the other about what happened fifteen years ago." He drew slowly on his pipe. "But who launched it, then? It had to be launched by somebody."

"Don't you think I've been tormenting myself with that question for the last fifteen years?" Pitov demanded. "You know, there were people inside the Soviet Union — not many, and they kept themselves well hidden — who were dedicated to the overthrow of the Soviet regime. They, or some of them, might have thought that the devastation of both our countries, and the obliteration of civilization in the Northern Hemisphere, would be a cheap price to pay for ending the rule of the Communist Party."

"Could they have built an ICBM with a thermonuclear warhead in secret?" he asked. "There were also fanatical nationalist groups in Europe, both sides of the Iron Curtain, who might have thought our mutual destruction would be worth the risks involved."

"There was China, and India. If your country and mine wiped each other out, they could go back to the old ways and the old traditions. Or Japan, or the Moslem States. In the end, they all went down along with us, but what criminal ever expects to fall?"

"We have too many suspects, and the trail's too cold, Alexis. That rocket wouldn't have had to have been launched anywhere in the Northern Hemisphere. For instance, our friends here in the Argentine have been doing very well by themselves since *El Coloso del Norte* went down."

And there were the Australians, picking themselves up bargains in real-estate in the East Indies at gun-point, and there were the Boers, trekking north again, in tanks instead of ox-wagons. And Brazil, with a not-too-implausible pretender to the Braganza throne, calling itself the Portuguese Empire and looking eastward. And, to complete the picture, here were Professor Doctor Lee Richardson and Comrade Professor Alexis Petrovitch Pitov, getting ready to test a missile with a matter-annihilation warhead.

No. This thing just wasn't a weapon.

A jeep came around the corner, lighting the dark roadway between the bungalows, its radio on and counting down — *Twenty two minutes. Twenty one fifty nine, fifty eight, fifty seven* — It came to a stop in front of their bungalow, at exactly Minus Two Hours, Twenty One Minutes, Fifty Four Seconds. The driver called out in Spanish:

"Doctor Richardson; Doctor Pitov! Are you ready?"

"Yes, ready. We're coming."

They both got to their feet, Richardson pulling himself up reluctantly. The older you get, the harder it is to leave a comfortable chair. He settled himself beside his colleague and former enemy, and the jeep started again, rolling between the buildings of the living-quarters area and out onto the long, straight road across the pampas toward the distant blaze of electric lights.

He wondered why he had been thinking so much, lately, about the Auburn Bomb. He'd questioned, at times, indignantly, of course, whether Russia had launched it — but it wasn't until tonight, until he had heard what Pitov had had to say, that he seriously doubted it. Pitov wouldn't lie about it, and Pitov would have been in a position to have known the truth, if the missile had been launched from Russia. Then he stopped thinking about what was water — or blood — a long time over the dam.

The special policeman at the entrance to the launching site reminded them that they were both smoking; when they extinguished, respectively, their cigarette and pipe, he waved the jeep on and went back to his argument with a carload of tourists who wanted to get a good view of the launching.

"There, now, Lee; do you need anything else to convince you that this isn't a weapon project?" Pitov asked.

"No, now that you mention it. I don't. You know, I don't believe I've had to show an identity card the whole time I've been here."

"I don't believe I have an identity card," Pitov said. "Think of that."

The lights blazed everywhere around them, but mostly about the rocket that towered above everything else, so thick that it seemed squat. The gantry-cranes had been hauled away, now, and it stood alone, but it was still wreathed in thick electric cables. They were pouring enough current into that thing to light half the street-lights in Buenos Aires; when the cables were blown free by separation charges at the blastoff, the generators powered by the rocket-engines had better be able to take over, because if the magnetic field collapsed and that fifty-kilo chunk of negative-proton matter came in contact with natural positive-proton matter, an old-fashioned H-bomb would be a firecracker to what would happen. Just one hundred kilos of pure, two-hundred proof MC2.

The driver took them around the rocket, dodging assorted trucks and mobile machinery that were being hurried out of the way. The countdown was just beyond two hours five minutes. The jeep stopped at the edge of a crowd around three more trucks, and Doctor Eugenio Galvez, the director of the Institute, left the crowd and approached at an awkward half-run as they got down.

"Is everything checked, gentlemen?" he wanted to know.

"It was this afternoon at 1730," Pitov told him. "And nobody's been burning my telephone to report anything different. Are the balloons and the drone planes ready?"

"The Air Force just finished checking; they're ready.

Captain Urquiola flew one of the planes over the course and made a guidance-tape; that's been duplicated and all the planes are equipped with copies."

"How's the wind?" Richardson asked.

"Still steady. We won't have any trouble about fallout or with the balloons."

"Then we'd better go back to the bunker and make sure everybody there is on the job."

The loudspeaker was counting down to Two Hours One Minute.

"Could you spare a few minutes to talk to the press?" Eugenio Galvez asked. "And perhaps say a few words for telecast? This last is most important; we can't explain too many times the purpose of this experiment. There is still much hostility, arising from fear that we are testing a nuclear weapon."

The press and telecast services were well represented; there were close to a hundred correspondents, from all over South America, from South Africa and Australia, even one from Ceylon. They had three trucks, with mobile telecast pickups, and when they saw who was approaching, they released the two rocketry experts they had been quizzing and pounced on the new victims.

Was there any possibility that negative-proton matter might be used as a weapon?

"Anything can be used as a weapon; you could stab a man to death with that lead pencil you're using," Pitov replied. "But I doubt if negamatter will ever be so used. We're certainly not working on weapons design here. We started, six years ago, with the ability to produce negative protons, reverse-spin neutrons, and positrons, and the theoretical possibility of assembling them into negamatter. We have just gotten a fifty kilogramme mass of nega-iron assembled. In those six years, we had to invent all our techniques, and design all our equipment. If we'd been insane enough to want to build a nuclear weapon, after what we went through up North, we could have done so from memory, and designed a better — which is to say a worse—one from memory in a few days."

"Yes, and building a negamatter bomb for military purposes would be like digging a fifty foot shaft to get a rock to bash somebody's head in, when you could do the job better with the shovel you're digging with," Richardson added. "The time, money, energy and work we put in on this thing would be ample to construct twenty thermonuclear bombs. And that's only a small part of it." He went on to tell them about the magnetic bottle inside the rocket's warhead, mentioning how much electric current was needed to keep up the magnetic field that insulated the negamatter from contact with posimatter.

"Then what was the purpose of this experiment, Doctor Richardson?"

"Oh, we were just trying to find out a few basic facts about natural structure. Long ago, it was realized that the nucleonic particles — protons, neutrons, mesons and so on — must have structure of their own. Since we started constructing negative-proton matter, we've found out a few things about nucleonic structure. Some rather odd things, including fractions of Planck's constant."

A couple of the correspondents — a man from La Prensa, and an Australian — whistled softly. The others looked blank. Pitov took over:

"You see, gentlemen, most of what we learned, we learned from putting negamatter atoms together. We annihilated a few of them — over there in that little concrete building, we have one of the most massive steel vaults in the world, where we do that — but we assembled millions of them for every one we annihilated, and that chunk of nega-iron inside the magnetic bottle kept growing. And when you have a piece of negamatter you don't want, you can't just throw it out on the scrap-pile. We might have rocketed it into escape velocity and let it blow up in space, away from the Moon or any of the artificial satellites, but why waste it? So we're going to have the rocket eject it, and when it falls, we can see, by our telemetered instruments, just what happens."

"Well, won't it be annihilated by contact with atmosphere?" somebody asked.

"That's one of the things we want to find out," Pitov said. "We estimate about twenty percent loss from contact with atmosphere, but the mass that actually lands on the target area should be about forty kilos. It should be something of a spectacle, coming down."

"You say you had to assemble it, after creating the negative protons and neutrons and the positrons. Doesn't any of this sort of matter exist in nature?"

The man who asked that knew better himself. He just wanted the answer on the record.

"Oh no; not on this planet, and probably not in the Galaxy. There may be whole galaxies composed of nothing but negamatter. There may even be isolated stars and planetary systems inside our Galaxy composed of negamatter, though I think that very improbable. But when negamatter and posimatter come into contact with one another, the result is immediate mutual annihilation."

They managed to get away from the press, and returned as far as the bunkers, a mile and a half away. Before they went inside, Richardson glanced up at the sky, fixing the location of a few of the more conspicuous stars in his mind. There were almost a hundred men and women inside, each at his or her instruments — view-screens, radar indicators, detection instruments of a dozen kinds. The reporters and telecast people arrived shortly afterward, and Eugenio Galvez took them in tow. While Richardson and Pitov were making their last-minute rounds, the countdown progressed past minus one hour, and at minus twenty minutes all the overhead lights went off and the small instrument operators' lights came on.

Pitov turned on a couple of view-screens, one from a pickup on the roof of the bunker and another from the launching-pad. They sat down side by side and waited. Richardson got his pipe out and began loading it. The loudspeaker was saying: *"Minus two minutes, one fifty nine, fifty eight, fifty seven —"*

He let his mind drift away from the test, back to the world that had been smashed around his ears in the autumn of 1969. He was doing that so often, now, when he should be thinking about —

"Two seconds, one second. FIRING!"

It was a second later that his eyes focussed on the left hand view-screen. Red and yellow flames were gushing out at the bottom of the rocket, and it was beginning to tremble. Then the upper jets, the ones that furnished power for the generators, began firing. He looked anxiously at the meters; the generators were building up power. Finally, when he was sure that the rocket would be blasting off anyhow, the separator-charges fired and the heavy cables fell away. An instant later, the big missile started inching upward, gaining speed by the second, first slowly and jerkily and then more rapidly, until it passed out of the field of the pickup. He watched the rising spout of fire from the other screen until it passed from sight.

By that time, Pitov had twisted a dial and gotten another view on the left hand screen, this time from close to the target. That camera was radar-controlled; it had fastened onto the approaching missile, which was still invisible. The stars swung slowly across the screen until Richardson recognized the ones he had spotted at the zenith. In a moment, now, the rocket, a hundred miles overhead, would be nosing down, and then the warhead would open and the magnetic field inside would alter and the mass of negamatter would be ejected.

The stars were blotted out by a sudden glow of light.

Even at a hundred miles, there was enough atmospheric density to produce considerable energy release. Pitov, beside him, was muttering, partly in German and partly in Russian; most of what Richardson caught was figures. Trying to calculate how much of the mass of unnatural iron would get down for the ground blast. Then the right hand screen broke into a wriggling orgy of color, and at the same time every scrap of radio-transmitted apparatus either went out or began reporting erratically. The left hand screen, connected by wiring to the pickup on the roof, was still functioning. For a moment, Richardson wondered what was going on, and then shocked recognition drove that from his mind as he stared at the ever-brightening glare in the sky.

It was the Auburn Bomb again! He was back, in memory, to the night on the shore of Lake Ontario; the party breaking up in the early hours of morning; he and Janet and the people with whom they had been spending a vacation week standing on the lawn as the guests were getting into their cars. And then the sudden light in the sky. The cries of surprise, and then of alarm as it seemed to be rushing straight down upon them. He and Janet, clutching each other and staring up in terror at the falling blaze from which there seemed no escape. Then relief, as it curved away from them and fell to the south. And then the explosion, lighting the whole southern sky.

There was a similar explosion in the screen, when the mass of nega-iron landed — a sheet of pure white light, so bright and so quick as to almost pass above the limit of visibility, and then a moment's darkness that was in his stunned eyes more than in the screen, and then the rising glow of updrawn incandescent dust.

Before the sound-waves had reached them, he had been legging it into the house. The television had been on, and it had been acting as insanely as the screen on his right now. He had called the State Police — the telephones had been working all right — and told them who he was, and they had told him to stay put and they'd send a car for him. They did, within minutes. Janet and his host and hostess had waited with him on the lawn until it came, and after he had gotten into it, he had turned around and looked back through the rear window, and seen Janet standing under the front light, holding the little dog in her arms, flopping one of its silly little paws up and down with her hand to wave goodbye to him.

He had seen her and the dog like that every day of his life for the last fifteen years.

"What kind of radiation are you getting?" he could hear Alexis Pitov asking into a phone. "What? Nothing else? Oh; yes, of course. But mostly cosmic. That shouldn't last long." He turned from the phone. "A devil's own dose of cosmic, and some gamma. It was the cosmic radiation that put the radios and telescreens out. That's why I insisted that the drone planes be independent of radio control."

They always got cosmic radiation from the micro-annihilations in the test-vault. Well, now they had an idea of what produced natural cosmic rays. There must be quite a bit of negamatter and posimatter going into mutual annihilation and total energy release through the Universe.

"Of course, there were no detectors set up in advance around Auburn," he said. "We didn't really begin to find anything out for half an hour. By that time, the cosmic radiation was over and we weren't getting anything but gamma."

"What — What has Auburn to do — ?" The Russian stopped short. "You think this was the same thing?" He gave it a moment's consideration. "Lee, you're crazy! There wasn't an atom of artificial negamatter in the world in 1969. Nobody had made any before us. We gave each other some scientific surprises, then, but nobody surprised both of us. You and I, between us, knew everything that was going on in nuclear physics in the world. And you know as well as I do —"

A voice came out of the public-address speaker. "Some of the radio equipment around the target area, that wasn't knocked out by blast, is beginning to function again. There is an increasingly heavy gamma radiation, but no more cosmic rays. They were all prompt radiation from the annihilation; the gamma is secondary effect. Wait a moment; Captain Urquiola, of the Air Force, says that the first drone plane is about to take off."

It had been two hours after the blast that the first drones had gone over what had been Auburn, New York. He was trying to remember, as exactly as possible, what had been learned from them. Gamma radiation; a great deal of gamma. But it didn't last long. It had been almost down to a safe level by the time the investigation had been called off, and, two months after there had been no more missiles, and no way of producing more, and no targets to send them against if they'd had them, rather — he had been back at Auburn on his hopeless quest, and there had been almost no trace of radiation. Nothing but a wide, shallow crater, almost two hundred feet in diameter and only fifteen at its deepest, already full of water, and a circle of flattened and scattered rubble for a mile and a half all around it. He was willing to bet anything that that was what they'd find where the chunk of nega-iron had landed, fifty miles away on the pampas.

Well, the first drone ought to be over the target area before long, and at least one of the balloons that had been sent up was reporting its course by radio. The radios in the others were silent, and the recording counters had probably jammed in all of them. There'd be something of interest when the first drone came back. He dragged his mind back to the present, and went to work with Alexis Pitov.

They were at it all night, checking, evaluating, making sure that the masses of data that were coming in were being promptly processed for programming the computers. At each of the increasingly frequent coffee-breaks, he noticed Pitov looking curiously. He said nothing, however, until, long after dawn, they stood outside the bunker, waiting for the jeep that would take them back to their bungalow and watching the line of trucks — Argentine army engineers, locally hired laborers, load after load of prefab-huts and equipment — going down toward the target-area, where they would be working for the next week.

"Lee, were you serious?" Pitov asked. "I mean, about this being like the one at Auburn?"

"It was exactly like Auburn; even that blazing light that came rushing down out of the sky. I wondered about that at the time — what kind of a missile would produce an effect like that. Now I know. We just launched one like it."

"But that's impossible! I told you, between us we know everything that was happening in nuclear physics then. Nobody in the world knew how to assemble atoms of negamatter and build them into masses."

"Nobody, and nothing, on this planet built that mass of negamatter. I doubt if it even came from this Galaxy. But we didn't know that, then. When that negamatter meteor fell, the only thing anybody could think of was that it had been a Soviet missile. If it had hit around Leningrad or Moscow or Kharkov, who would you have blamed it on?"

FLIGHT FROM TOMORROW

1

But yesterday, a whole planet had shouted: *Hail Hradzka! Hail the Leader!* Today, they were screaming: *Death to Hradzka! Kill the tyrant!*

The Palace, where Hradzka, surrounded by his sycophants and guards, had lorded it over a solar system, was now an inferno. Those who had been too closely identified with the dictator's rule to hope for forgiveness were fighting to the last, seeking only a quick death in combat; one by one, their isolated points of resistance were being wiped out. The corridors and chambers of the huge palace were thronged with rebels, loud with their shouts, and with the rasping hiss of heat-beams and the crash of blasters, reeking with the stench of scorched plastic and burned flesh, of hot metal and charred fabric. The living quarters were overrun; the mob smashed down walls and tore up floors in search of secret hiding-places. They found strange things—the space-ship that had been built under one of the domes, in readiness for flight to the still-loyal colonies on Mars or the Asteroid Belt, for instance—but Hradzka himself they could not find.

At last, the search reached the New Tower which reared its head five thousand feet above the palace, the highest thing in the city. They blasted down the huge steel doors, cut the power from the energy-screens. They landed from antigrav-cars on the upper levels. But except for barriers of metal and concrete and energy, they met with no opposition. Finally, they came to the spiral stairway which led up to the great metal sphere which capped the whole structure.

General Zarvas, the Army Commander who had placed himself at the head of the revolt, stood with his foot on the lowest step, his followers behind him. There was Prince Burvanny, the leader of the old nobility, and Ghorzesko Orhm, the merchant, and between them stood Tobbh, the chieftain of the mutinous slaves. There were clerks; laborers; poor but haughty nobles: and wealthy merchants who had long been forced to hide their riches from the dictator's tax-gatherers, and soldiers, and spacemen.

"You'd better let some of us go first sir," General Zarvas' orderly, a blood-stained bandage about his head, his uniform in rags, suggested. "You don't know what might be up there."

The General shook his head. "I'll go first." Zarvas Pol was not the man to send subordinates into danger ahead of himself. "To tell the truth, I'm afraid we won't find anything at all up there."

"You mean. . . ?" Ghorzesko Orhm began.

"The 'time-machine'," Zarvas Pol replied. "If he's managed to get it finished, the Great Mind only knows where he may be, now. Or when."

He loosened the blaster in his holster and started up the long spiral. His followers spread out, below; sharpshooters took position to cover his ascent. Prince Burvanny and Tobbh the Slave started to follow him. They hesitated as each motioned the other to precede him; then the nobleman followed the general, his blaster drawn, and the brawny slave behind him.

The door at the top was open, and Zarvas Pol stepped through but there was nothing in the great spherical room except a raised dais some fifty feet in diameter, its polished metal top strangely clean and empty. And a crumpled heap of burned cloth and charred flesh that had, not long ago, been a man. An old man with a white beard, and the seven-pointed star of the Learned Brothers on his breast, advanced to meet the armed intruders.

"So he is gone, Kradzy Zago?" Zarvas Pol said, holstering his weapon. "Gone in the 'time-machine', to hide in yesterday or tomorrow. And you let him go?"

The old one nodded. "He had a blaster, and I had none." He indicated the body on the floor. "Zoldy Jarv had no blaster, either, but he tried to stop Hradzka. See, he squandered his life as a fool squanders his money, getting nothing for it. And a man's life is not money, Zarvas Pol."

"I do not blame you, Kradzy Zago," General Zarvas said. "But now you must get to work, and build us another 'time-machine', so that we can hunt him down."

"Does revenge mean so much to you, then?"

The soldier made an impatient gesture. "Revenge is for fools, like that pack of screaming beasts below. I do not kill for revenge; I kill because dead men do no harm."

"Hradzka will do us no more harm," the old scientist replied. "He is a thing of yesterday; of a time long past and half-lost in the mists of legend."

"No matter. As long as he exists, at any point in space-time, Hradzka is still a threat. Revenge means much to Hradzka; he will return for it, when we least expect him."

The old man shook his head. "No, Zarvas Pol, Hradzka will not return."

Hradzka holstered his blaster, threw the switch that sealed the "time-machine", put on the antigrav-unit and started the time-shift unit. He reached out and set the destination-dial for the mid-Fifty-Second Century of the Atomic Era. That would land him in the Ninth Age of Chaos, following the Two-Century War and the collapse of the World Theocracy. A good time for his purpose: the world would be slipping back into barbarism, and yet possess the technologies of former civilizations. A hundred little national states would be trying to regain social stability, competing and warring with one another. Hradzka glanced back over his shoulder at the cases of books, record-spools, tri-dimensional pictures, and scale-models. These people of the past would welcome him and his science of the future, would make him their leader.

He would start in a small way, by taking over the local feudal or tribal government, would arm his followers with weapons of the future. Then he would impose his rule upon neighboring tribes, or princedoms, or communes, or whatever, and build a strong sovereignty; from that he envisioned a world empire, a Solar System empire.

Then, he would build "time-machines", many "time-machines". He would recruit an army such as the universe had never seen, a swarm of men from every age in the past. At that point, he would return to the Hundredth Century of the Atomic Era, to wreak vengeance upon those who had risen against him. A slow smile grew on Hradzka's thin lips as he thought of the tortures with which he would put Zarvas Pol to death.

He glanced up at the great disc of the indicator and frowned. Already he was back to the year 7500, A.E., and the temporal-displacement had not begun to slow. The disc was turning even more rapidly—7000, 6000, 5500; he gasped slightly. Then he had passed his destination; he was now in the Fortieth Century, but the indicator was slowing. The hairline crossed the Thirtieth Century, the Twentieth, the Fifteenth, the Tenth. He wondered what had gone wrong, but he had recovered from his fright by this time. When this insane machine stopped, as it must around the First Century of the Atomic Era, he would investigate, make repairs, then shift forward to his target-point. Hradzka was determined upon the Fifty-Second Century; he had made a special study of the history of that period, had learned the language spoken then, and he understood the methods necessary to gain power over the natives of that time.

The indicator-disc came to a stop, in the First Century. He switched on the magnifier and leaned forward to look; he had emerged into normal time in the year 10 of the Atomic Era, a decade after the first uranium-pile had gone into operation, and seven years after the first atomic bombs had been exploded in warfare. The altimeter showed that he was hovering at eight thousand feet above ground-level.

Slowly, he cut out the antigrav, letting the "time machine" down easily. He knew that there had been no danger of materializing inside anything; the New Tower had been built to put it above anything that had occupied that space-point at any moment within history, or legend, or even the geological knowledge of man. What lay below, however, was uncertain. It was night—the visi-screen showed only a star-dusted, moonless-sky, and dark shadows below. He snapped another switch; for a few micro-seconds a beam of intense light was turned on, automatically photographing the landscape under him. A second later, the developed picture was projected upon another screen; it showed only wooded mountains and a barren, brush-grown valley.

The "time-machine" came to rest with a soft jar and a crashing of broken bushes that was audible through the sound pickup. Hradzka pulled the main switch; there was a click as the shielding went out and the door opened. A breath of cool night air drew into the hollow sphere.

Then there was a loud *bang* inside the mechanism, and a flash of blue-white light which turned to pinkish flame with a nasty crackling. Curls of smoke began to rise from the square black box that housed the "time-shift" mechanism, and from behind the instrument-board. In a moment, everything was glowing-hot: driblets of aluminum and silver were running down from the instruments. Then the whole interior of the "time-machine" was afire; there was barely time for Hradzka to leap through the open door.

The brush outside impeded him, and he used his blaster to clear a path for himself away from the big sphere, which was now glowing faintly on the outside. The heat grew in intensity, and the brush outside was taking fire. It was not until he had gotten two hundred yards from the machine that he stopped, realizing what had happened.

The machine, of course, had been sabotaged. That would have been young Zoldy, whom he had killed, or that old billy-goat, Kradzy Zago; the latter, most likely. He cursed both of them for having marooned him in this savage age, at the very beginning of atomic civilization, with all his printed and recorded knowledge destroyed. Oh, he could still gain mastery over these barbarians; he knew enough to fashion a crude blaster, or a heat-beam gun, or an atomic-electric conversion unit. But without his books and records, he could never build an antigrav unit, and the secret of the "temporal shift" was lost.

For "Time" is not an object, or a medium which can be travelled along. The "Time-Machine" was not a vehicle; it was a mechanical process of displacement within the space-time continuum, and those who constructed it knew that it could not be used with the sort of accuracy that the dials indicated. Hradzka had ordered his scientists to produce a "Time Machine", and they had combined the possible—displacement within the space-time continuum—with the sort of fiction the dictator demanded, for their own well-being. Even had there been no sabotage, his return to his own "time" was nearly of zero probability.

The fire, spreading from the "time-machine", was

blowing toward him; he observed the wind-direction and hurried around out of the path of the flames. The light enabled him to pick his way through the brush, and, after crossing a small stream, he found a rutted road and followed it up the mountainside until he came to a place where he could rest concealed until morning.

2

It was broad daylight when he woke, and there was a strange throbbing sound; Hradzka lay motionless under the brush where he had slept, his blaster ready. In a few minutes, a vehicle came into sight, following the road down the mountainside.

It was a large thing, four-wheeled, with a projection in front which probably housed the engine and a cab for the operator. The body of the vehicle was simply an open rectangular box. There were two men in the cab, and about twenty or thirty more crowded into the box body. These were dressed in faded and nondescript garments of blue and gray and brown; all were armed with crude weapons—axes, bill-hooks, long-handled instruments with serrated edges, and what looked like broad-bladed spears. The vehicle itself, which seemed to be propelled by some sort of chemical-explosion engine, was dingy and mud-splattered; the men in it were ragged and unshaven. Hradzka snorted in contempt; they were probably warriors of the local tribe, going to the fire in the belief that it had been started by raiding enemies. When they found the wreckage of the "time-machine", they would no doubt believe that it was the chariot of some god and drag it home to be venerated.

A plan of action was taking shape in his mind. First, he must get clothing of the sort worn by these people, and find a safe hiding-place for his own things. Then, pretending to be a deaf-mute, he would go among them to learn something of their customs and pick up the language. When he had done that, he would move on to another tribe or village, able to tell a credible story for himself. For a while, it would be necessary for him to do menial work, but in the end, he would establish himself among these people. Then he could gather around him a faction of those who were dissatisfied with whatever conditions existed, organize a conspiracy, make arms for his followers, and start his program of power-seizure.

The matter of clothing was attended to shortly after he had crossed the mountain and descended into the valley on the other side. Hearing a clinking sound some distance from the road, as of metal striking stone, Hradzka stole cautiously through the woods until he came within sight of a man who was digging with a mattock, uprooting small bushes of a particular sort, with rough gray bark and three-pointed leaves. When he had dug one up, he would cut off the roots and then slice away the root-bark with a knife, putting it into a sack. Hradzka's lip curled contemptuously; the fellow was gathering the stuff for medicinal use. He had heard of the use of roots and herbs for such purposes by the ancient savages.

The blaster would be no use here; it was too powerful, and would destroy the clothing that the man was wearing. He unfastened a strap from his belt and attached it to a stone to form a hand-loop, then, inched forward behind the lone herb-gatherer. When he was close enough, he straightened and rushed forward, swinging his improvised weapon. The man heard him and turned, too late.

After undressing his victim, Hradzka used the mattock to finish him, and then to dig a grave. The fugitive buried his own clothes with the murdered man, and donned the faded blue shirt, rough shoes, worn trousers and jacket.

The blaster he concealed under the jacket, and he kept a few other Hundredth Century gadgets; these he would hide somewhere closer to his center of operations.

He had kept, among other things, a small box of food-concentrate capsules, and in one pocket of the newly acquired jacket he found a package containing food. It was rough and unappetizing fare—slices of cold cooked meat between slices of some cereal substance. He ate these before filling in the grave, and put the paper wrappings in with the dead man. Then, his work finished, he threw the mattock into the brush and set out again, grimacing disgustedly and scratching himself. The clothing he had appropriated was verminous.

Crossing another mountain, he descended into a second valley, and, for a time, lost his way among a tangle of narrow ravines. It was dark by the time he mounted a hill and found himself looking down another valley, in which a few scattered lights gave evidence of human habitations. Not wishing to arouse suspicion by approaching these in the night-time, he found a place among some young evergreens where he could sleep.

The next morning, having breakfasted on a concentrate capsule, he found a hiding-place for his blaster in a hollow tree. It was in a sufficiently prominent position so that he could easily find it again, and at the same time unlikely to be discovered by some native. Then he went down into the inhabited valley.

He was surprised at the ease with which he established contact with the natives. The first dwelling which he approached, a cluster of farm-buildings at the upper end of the valley, gave him shelter. There was a man, clad in the same sort of rough garments Hradzka had taken from the body of the herb-gatherer, and a woman in a faded and shapeless dress. The man was thin and work-bent; the woman short and heavy. Both were past middle age.

He made inarticulate sounds to attract their attention, then gestured to his mouth and ears to indicate his assumed affliction. He rubbed his stomach to portray hunger. Looking about, he saw an ax sticking in a chopping-block, and a pile of wood near it, probably the fuel used by these people. He took the ax, split up some of the wood, then repeated the hunger-signs. The man and the woman both nodded, laughing; he was shown a pile of tree-limbs, and the man picked up a short billet of wood and used it like a measuring-rule, to indicate that all the wood was to be cut to that length.

Hradzka fell to work, and by mid-morning, he had all the wood cut. He had seen a circular stone, mounted on a trestle with a metal axle through it, and judged it to be some sort of a grinding-wheel, since it was fitted with a foot-pedal and a rusty metal can was set above it to spill water onto the grinding-edge. After chopping the wood, he carefully sharpened the ax, handing it to the man for inspection. This seemed to please the man; he clapped Hradzka on the shoulder, making commendatory sounds.

It required considerable time and ingenuity to make himself a more or less permanent member of the household. Hradzka had made a survey of the farmyard, noting the sorts of work that would normally be performed on the farm, and he pantomimed this work in its simpler operations. He pointed to the east, where the sun would rise, and to the zenith, and to the west. He made signs indicative of eating, and of sleeping, and of rising, and of working. At length, he succeeded in conveying his meaning.

There was considerable argument between the man and the woman, but his proposal was accepted, as he expected that it would. It was easy to see that the work of the farm was hard for this aging couple; now, for a place to sleep and a little food, they were able to acquire a strong and intelligent slave.

In the days that followed, he made himself useful to the farm people; he fed the chickens and the livestock, milked the cow, worked in the fields. He slept in a small room at the top of the house, under the eaves, and ate with the man and woman in the farmhouse kitchen.

It was not long before he picked up a few words which he had heard his employers using, and related them to the things or acts spoken of. And he began to notice that these people, in spite of the crudities of their own life, enjoyed some of the advantages of a fairly complex civilization. Their implements were not hand-craft products, but showed machine workmanship. There were two objects hanging on hooks on the kitchen wall which he was sure were weapons. Both had wooden shoulder-stocks, and wooden fore-pieces; they had long tubes extending to the front, and triggers like blasters. One had double tubes mounted side-by-side, and double triggers; the other had an octagonal tube mounted over a round tube, and a loop extension on the trigger-guard. Then, there was a box on the kitchen wall, with a mouthpiece and a cylindrical tube on a cord. Sometimes a bell would ring out of the box, and the woman would go to this instrument, take down the tube and hold it to her ear, and talk into the mouthpiece. There was another box from which voices would issue, of people conversing, or of orators, or of singing, and some-times instrumental music. None of these were objects made by savages; these people probably traded with some fairly high civilization. They were not illiterate; he found printed matter, indicating the use of some phonetic alphabet, and paper pamphlets containing printed repro-ductions of photographs as well as verbal text.

There was also a vehicle on the farm, powered, like the one he had seen on the road, by an engine in which a hydrocarbon liquid-fuel was exploded. He made it his business to examine this minutely, and to study its construction and operation until he was thoroughly familiar with it.

It was not until the third day after his arrival that the chickens began to die. In the morning, Hradzka found three of them dead when he went to feed them, the rest drooping unhealthily; he summoned the man and showed him what he had found. The next morning, they were all dead, and the cow was sick. She gave bloody milk, that evening, and the next morning she lay in her stall and would not get up.

The man and the woman were also beginning to sicken, though both of them tried to continue their work. It was the woman who first noticed that the plants around the farmhouse were withering and turning yellow.

The farmer went to the stable with Hradzka and looked at the cow. Shaking his head, he limped back to the house, and returned carrying one of the weapons from the kitchen—the one with the single trigger and the octagonal tube. As he entered the stable, he jerked down and up on the loop extension of the trigger-guard, then put the weapon to his shoulder and pointed it at the cow. It made a flash, and roared louder even than a hand-blaster, and the cow jerked convulsively and was dead. The man then indicated by signs that Hradzka was to drag the dead cow out of the stable, dig a hole, and bury it. This Hradzka did, carefully examining the wound in the cow's head—the weapon, he decided, was not an energy-weapon, but a simple solid-missile projector.

By evening, neither the man nor the woman were able to eat, and both seemed to be suffering intensely. The man used the communicating-instrument on the wall, probably calling on his friends for help. Hradzka did what he could to make them comfortable, cooked his own meal, washed the dishes as he had seen the woman doing, and tidied up the kitchen.

It was not long before people, men and women whom he had seen on the road or who had stopped at the farmhouse while he had been there, began arriving, some - carrying baskets of food; and shortly after Hradzka had eaten, a vehicle like the farmer's, but in better condition and of better quality, arrived and a young man got out of it and entered the house, carrying a leather bag. He was apparently some sort of a scientist; he examined the man and his wife, asked many questions, and administered drugs. He also took samples for blood-tests and urinalysis. This, Hradzka considered, was another of the many contradictions he had encountered among these people—this man behaved like an educated scientist, and seemingly had nothing in common with the peasant herb-gatherer on the mountainside.

The fact was that Hradzka was worried. The strange death of the animals, the blight which had smitten the trees and vegetables around the farm, and the sickness of the farmer and his woman, all mystified him. He did not know of any disease which would affect plants and animals and humans; he wondered if some poisonous gas might not be escaping from the earth near the farmhouse. However, he had not, himself, been affected. He also disliked the way in which the doctor and the neighbors seemed to be talking about him. While he had come to a considerable revision of his original opinion about the culture-level of these people, it was not impossible that they might suspect him of having caused the whole thing by witchcraft; at any moment, they might fall upon him and put him to death. In any case, there was no longer any use in his staying here, and it might be wise if he left at once.

Accordingly, he filled his pockets with food from the pantry and slipped out of the farmhouse; before his absence was discovered he was well on his way down the road.

3

That night, Hradzka slept under a bridge across a fairly wide stream; the next morning, he followed the road until he came to a town. It was not a large place; there were perhaps four or five hundred houses and other buildings in it. Most of these were dwellings like the farmhouse where he had been staying, but some were much larger, and seemed to be places of business. One of these latter was a concrete structure with wide doors at the front; inside, he could see men working on the internal-combustion vehicles which seemed to be in almost universal use. Hradzka decided to obtain employment here.

It would be best, he decided, to continue his pretense of being a deaf-mute. He did not know whether a world-language were in use at this time or not, and even if not, the pretense of being a foreigner unable to speak the local dialect might be dangerous. So he entered the vehicle-repair shop and accosted a man in a clean shirt who seemed to be issuing instructions to the workers, going into his pantomime of the homeless mute seeking employment.

The master of the repair-shop merely laughed at him, however. Hradzka became more insistent in his manner, making signs to indicate his hunger and willingness to work. The other men in the shop left their tasks and gathered around; there was much laughter and unmistakably ribald and derogatory remarks. Hradzka was beginning to give up hope of getting employment here when one of the workmen approached the master and whispered something to him.

The two of them walked away, conversing in low voices. Hradzka thought he understood the situation; no doubt the workman, thinking to lighten his own labor, was urging that the vagrant be employed, for no other pay than food and lodging. At length, the master assented to his employee's urgings; he returned, showed Hradzka a hose and a bucket and sponges and cloths, and set him to work cleaning the mud from one of the vehicles. Then, after seeing that the work was being done properly, he went away, entering a room at one side of the shop.

About twenty minutes later, another man entered the shop. He was not dressed like any of the other people whom Hradzka had seen; he wore a gray tunic and breeches, polished black boots, and a cap with a visor and a metal insignia on it; on a belt, he carried a holstered weapon like a blaster.

After speaking to one of the workers, who pointed Hradzka out to him, he approached the fugitive and said something. Hradzka made gestures at his mouth and ears and made gargling sounds; the newcomer shrugged and motioned him to come with him, at the same time producing a pair of handcuffs from his belt and jingling them suggestively.

In a few seconds, Hradzka tried to analyze the situation and estimate its possibilities. The newcomer was a soldier, or, more likely, a policeman, since manacles were a part of his equipment. Evidently, since the evening before, a warning had been made public by means of communicating devices such as he had seen at the farm, advising people that a man of his description, pretending to be a deaf-mute, should be detained and the police notified; it had been for that reason that the workman had persuaded his master to employ Hradzka. No doubt he would be accused of causing the conditions at the farm by sorcery.

Hradzka shrugged and nodded, then went to the watertap to turn off the hose he had been using. He disconnected it, coiled it and hung it up, and then picked up the water-bucket. Then, without warning, he hurled the water into the policeman's face, sprang forward, swinging the bucket by the bale, and hit the man on the head. Releasing his grip on the bucket, he tore the blaster or whatever it was from the holster.

One of the workers swung a hammer, as though to throw it. Hradzka aimed the weapon at him and pulled the trigger; the thing belched fire and kicked back painfully in his hand, and the man fell. He used it again to drop the policeman, then thrust it into the waistband of his trousers and ran outside. The thing was not a blaster at all, he realized—only a missile-projector like the big weapons at the farm, utilizing the force of some chemical explosive.

The policeman's vehicle was standing outside. It was a small, single-seat, two wheeled affair. Having become familiar with the principles of these hydro-carbon engines from examination of the vehicle of the farm, and accustomed as he was to far more complex mechanisms than this crude affair, Hradzka could see at a glance how to operate it. Springing onto the saddle, he kicked away the folding support and started the engine. Just as he did, the master of the repair-shop ran outside, one of the small hand-weapons in his hand, and fired several shots. They all missed, but Hradzka heard the whining sound of the missiles passing uncomfortably close to him.

It was imperative that he recover the blaster he had hidden in the hollow tree at the head of the valley. By this time, there would be a concerted search under way for him, and he needed a better weapon than the solid-missile projector he had taken from the policeman. He did not know how many shots the thing contained, but if it propelled solid missiles by chemical explosion, there could not have been more than five or six such charges in the cylindrical part of the weapon which he had assumed to be the charge-holder. On the other hand, his blaster, a weapon of much greater power, contained enough energy for five hundred blasts, and with it were eight extra energy-capsules, giving him a total of four thousand five hundred blasts.

Handling the two-wheeled vehicle was no particular problem; although he had never ridden on anything of the sort before, it was child's play compared to controlling a Hundredth Century strato-rocket, and Hradzka was a skilled rocket-pilot.

Several times he passed vehicles on the road—the passenger vehicles with enclosed cabins, and cargo-vehicles piled high with farm produce. Once he encountered a large number of children, gathered in front of a big red building with a flagstaff in front, from which a queer flag, with horizontal red and white stripes and a white-spotted blue device in the corner, flew. They scattered off the road in terror at his approach; fortunately, he hit none of them, for at the speed at which he was traveling, such a collision would have wrecked his light vehicle.

As he approached the farm where he had spent the past few days, he saw two passenger-vehicles standing by the road. One was a black one, similar to the one in which the physician had come to the farm, and the other was white with black trimmings and bore the same device he had seen on the cap of the policeman. A policeman was sitting in the driver's seat of this vehicle, and another policeman was standing beside it, breathing smoke with one of the white paper cylinders these people used. In the farm-yard, two men were going about with a square black box; to this box, a tube was connected by a wire, and they were passing the tube about over the ground.

The policeman who was standing beside the vehicle saw him approach, and blew his whistle, then drew the weapon from his belt. Hradzka, who had been expecting some attempt to halt him, had let go the right-hand steering handle and drawn his own weapon; as the police-man drew, he fired at him. Without observing the effect of the shot, he sped on; before he had rounded the bend above the farm, several shots were fired after him.

A mile beyond, he came to the place where he had hidden the blaster. He stopped the vehicle and jumped off, plunging into the brush and racing toward the hollow tree. Just as he reached it, he heard a vehicle approach and stop, and the door of the police vehicle slam. Hradzka's fingers found the belt of his blaster; he dragged it out and buckled it on, tossing away the missile weapon he had been carrying.

Then, crouching behind the tree, he waited. A few moments later, he caught a movement in the brush to-ward the road. He brought up the blaster, aimed and squeezed the trigger. There was a faint bluish glow at the muzzle, and a blast of energy tore through the brush, smashing the molecular structure of everything that stood in the way. There was an involuntary shout of alarm from the direction of the road; at least one of the police-men had escaped the blast. Hradzka holstered his weapon and crept away for some distance, keeping under cover, then turned and waited for some sign of the presence of his enemies. For some time nothing happened; he de-cided to turn hunter against the men who were hunting him. He started back in the direction of the road, making a wide circle, flitting silently from rock to bush and from bush to tree, stopping often to look and listen.

This finally brought him upon one of the policemen, and almost terminated his flight at the same time. He must have grown over-confident and careless; suddenly a weapon roared, and a missile smashed through the brush inches from his face. The shot had come from his left and a little to the rear. Whirling, he blasted four times, in rapid succession, then turned and fled for a few yards, drop-ping and crawling behind a rock. When he looked back, he could see wisps of smoke rising from the shattered trees and bushes which had absorbed the energy-output of his weapon, and he caught a faint odor of burned flesh. One of his pursuers, at least, would pursue him no longer.

He slipped away, down into the tangle of ravines and hollows in which he had wandered the day before his arrival at the farm. For the time being, he felt safe, and finally confident that he was not being pursued, he stopped to rest. The place where he stopped seemed familiar, and he looked about. In a moment, he recognized the little stream, the pool where he had bathed his feet, the clump of seedling pines under which he had slept. He even found the silver-foil wrapping from the food concentrate capsule.

But there had been a change, since the night when he had slept here. Then the young pines had been green and alive; now they were blighted, and their needles had turned brown. Hradzka stood for a long time, looking at them. It was the same blight that had touched the plants around the farmhouse. And here, among the pine needles on the ground, lay a dead bird.

It took some time for him to admit, to himself, the implications of vegetation, the chickens, the cow, the farmer and his wife, had all sickened and died. He had been in this place, and now, when he had returned, he found that death had followed him here, too.

During the early centuries of the Atomic Era, he knew, there had been great wars, the stories of which had survived even to the Hundredth Century. Among the weapons that had been used, there had been artificial plagues and epidemics, caused by new types of bacteria developed in laboratories, against which the victims had possessed no protection. Those germs and viruses had persisted for centuries, and gradually had lost their power to harm mankind. Suppose, now, that he had brought some of them back with him, to a century before they had been developed. Suppose, that was, that he were a human plague-carrier. He thought of the vermin that had infested the clothing he had taken from the man he had killed on the other side of the mountain; they had not troubled him after the first day.

There was a throbbing mechanical sound somewhere in the air; he looked about, and finally identified its source. A small aircraft had come over the valley from the other side of the mountain and was circling lazily overhead. He froze, shrinking back under a pine-tree; as long as he remained motionless, he would not be seen, and soon the thing would go away. He was beginning to understand why the search for him was being pressed so relentlessly; as long as he remained alive, he was a menace to everybody in this First Century world.

He got out his supply of food concentrates, saw that he had only three capsules left, and put them away again. For a long time, he sat under the dying tree, chewing on a twig and thinking. There must be some way in which he could overcome, or even utilize, his inherent deadliness to these people. He might find some isolated community, conceal himself near it, invade it at night and infect it, and then, when everybody was dead, move in and take it for himself. But was there any such isolated community? The farmhouse where he had worked had been fairly remote, yet its inhabitants had been in communication with the outside world, and the physician had come immediately in response to their call for help.

The little aircraft had been circling overhead, directly above the place where he lay hidden. For a while, Hradzka was afraid it had spotted him, and was debating the advisability of using his blaster on it. Then it banked, turned and went away. He watched it circle over the valley on the other side of the mountain, and got to his feet.

4

Almost at once, there was a new sound—a multiple throbbing, at a quick, snarling tempo that hinted at enormous power, growing louder each second. Hradzka stiffened and drew his blaster; as he did, five more aircraft swooped over the crest of the mountain and came rushing down toward him; not aimlessly, but as though they knew exactly where he was. As they approached, the leading edges of their wings sparkled with light, branches began flying from the trees about him, and there was a loud hammering noise.

He aimed a little in front of them and began blasting. A wing flew from one of the aircraft, and it plunged downward. Another came apart in the air; a third burst into flames. The other two zoomed upward quickly. Hradzka swung his blaster after them, blasting again and again. He hit a fourth with a blast of energy, knocking it to pieces, and then the fifth was out of range. He blasted at it twice, but without effect; a hand-blaster was only good for a thousand yards at the most.

Holstering his weapon, he hurried away, following the stream and keeping under cover of trees. The last of the attacking aircraft had gone away, but the little scout-plane was still circling about, well out of blaster-range.

Once or twice, Hradzka was compelled to stay hidden for some time, not knowing the nature of the pilot's ability to detect him. It was during one of these waits that the next phase of the attack developed.

It began, like the last one, with a distant roar that swelled in volume until it seemed to fill the whole world. Then, fifteen or twenty thousand feet out of blaster-range, the new attackers swept into sight.

There must have been fifty of them, huge tapering things with wide-spread wings, flying in close formation, wave after V-shaped wave. He stood and stared at them, amazed; he had never imagined that such aircraft existed in the First Century. Then a high-pitched screaming sound cut through the roar of the propellers, and for an instant he saw countless small specks in the sky, falling downward. The first bomb-salvo landed in the young pines, where he had fought against the first air attack. Great gouts of flame shot upward, and smoke, and flying earth and debris. Hradzka turned and started to run. Another salvo fell in front of him; he veered to the left and plunged on through the undergrowth. Now the bombs were falling all about him, deafening him with their thunder, shaking him with concussion. He dodged, frightened, as the trunk of a tree came crashing down beside him. Then something hit him across the back, knocking him flat. For a moment, he lay stunned, then tried to rise. As he did, a searing light filled his eyes and a wave of intolerable heat swept over him. Then darkness. . . .

"No, Zarvas Pol," Kradzy Zago repeated. "Hradzka will not return; the 'time-machine' was sabotaged."

"So? By you?" the soldier asked.

The scientist nodded. "I knew the purpose for which he intended it. Hradzka was not content with having enslaved a whole Solar System: he hungered to bring tyranny and serfdom to all the past and all the future as well; he wanted to be master not only of the present but of the centuries that were and were to be, as well. I never took part in politics, Zarvas Pol; I had no hand in this revolt. But I could not be party to such a crime as Hradzka contemplated when it lay within my power to prevent it."

"The machine will take him out of our space-time continuum, or back to a time when this planet was a swirling cloud of flaming gas?" Zarvas Pol asked.

Kradzy Zago shook his head. "No, the unit is not powerful enough for that. It will only take him about ten thousand years into the past. But then, when it stops, the machine will destroy itself. It may destroy Hradzka with it or he may escape. But if he does, he will be left stranded ten thousand years ago, when he can do us no harm.

"Actually, it did not operate as he imagined and there is an infinitely small chance that he could have returned to our 'time', in any event. But I wanted to insure against even so small a chance."

"We can't be sure of that," Zarvas Pol objected. "He may know more about the machine than you think; enough more to build another like it. So you must build me a machine and I'll take back a party of volunteers and hunt him down."

"That would not be necessary, and you would only share his fate." Then, apparently changing the subject, Kradzy Zago asked: "Tell me, Zarvas Pol; have you never heard the legends of the Deadly Radiations?"

General Zarvas smiled. "Who has not? Every cadet at the Officers' College dreams of re-discovering them, to use as a weapon, but nobody ever has. We hear these tales of how, in the early days, atomic engines and piles and fission-bombs emitted particles which were utterly deadly, which would make anything with which they came in contact deadly, which would bring a horrible death to any human being. But these are only myths. All the ancient experiments have been duplicated time and again, and the deadly radiation effect has never been observed. Some say that it is a mere old-wives' terror tale; some say that the deaths were caused by fear of atomic energy, when it was still unfamiliar; others contend that the fundamental nature of atomic energy has altered by the degeneration of the fissionable matter. For my own part, I'm not enough of a scientist to have an opinion."

The old one smiled wanly. "None of these theories are correct. In the beginning of the Atomic Era, the Deadly Radiations existed. They still exist, but they are no longer deadly, because all life on this planet has adapted itself to such radiations, and all living things are now immune to them."

"And Hradzka has returned to a time when such immunity did not exist? But would that not be to his advantage?"

"Remember, General, that man has been using atomic energy for ten thousand years. Our whole world has become drenched with radioactivity. The planet, the seas, the atmosphere, and every living thing, are all radioactive, now. Radioactivity is as natural to us as the air we breathe. Now, you remember hearing of the great wars of the first centuries of the Atomic Era, in which whole nations were wiped out, leaving only hundreds of survivors out of millions. You, no doubt, think that such tales are products of ignorant and barbaric imagination, but I assure you, they are literally true. It was not the blast-effect of a few bombs which created such holocausts, but the radiations released by the bombs. And those who survived to carry on the race were men and women whose systems resisted the radiations, and they transmitted to their progeny that power of resistance. In many cases, their children were mutants—not monsters, although there were many of them, too, which did not survive—but humans who were immune to radioactivity."

"An interesting theory, Kradzy Zago," the soldier commented. "And one which conforms both to what we know of atomic energy and to the ancient legends. Then you would say that those radiations are still deadly—to the non-immune?"

"Exactly. And Hradzka, his body emitting those radiations, has returned to the First Century of the Atomic Era—to a world without immunity."

General Zarvas' smile vanished. "Man!" he cried in horror. "You have loosed a carrier of death among those innocent people of the past!"

Kradzy Zago nodded. "That is true. I estimate that Hradzka will probably cause the death of a hundred or so people, before he is dealt with. But dealt with he will be. Tell me, General; if a man should appear now, out of nowhere, spreading a strange and horrible plague wherever he went, what would you do?"

"Why, I'd hunt him down and kill him," General Zarvas replied. "Not for anything he did, but for the menace he was. And then, I'd cover his body with a mass of concrete bigger than this palace."

"Precisely." Kradzy Zago smiled. "And the military commanders and political leaders of the First Century were no less ruthless or efficient than you. You know how atomic energy was first used? There was an ancient nation, upon the ruins of whose cities we have built our own, which was famed for its idealistic humanitarianism. Yet that nation, treacherously attacked, created the first atomic bombs in self defense, and used them. It is among the people of that nation that Hradzka has emerged."

"But would they recognize him as the cause of the calamity he brings among them?"

"Of course. He will emerge at the time when atomic energy is first being used. They will have detectors for the Deadly Radiations—detectors we know nothing of, today, for a detection instrument must be free from the thing it is intended to detect, and today everything is radioactive. It will be a day or so before they discover what is happening to them, and not a few will die in that time, I fear; but once they have found out what is killing their people, Hradzka's days—no, his hours—will be numbered."

"A mass of concrete bigger than this place," Tobbh the Slave repeated General Zarvas' words. *"The Ancient Spaceport!"*

Prince Burvanny clapped him on the shoulder. "Tobbh, man! You've hit it!"

"You mean. . . ?" Kradzy Zago began.

"Yes. You all know of it. It's stood for nobody knows how many millennia, and nobody's ever decided what it was, to begin with, except that somebody, once, filled a valley with concrete, level from mountain-top to mountain-top. The accepted theory is that it was done for a firing-stand for the first Moon-rocket. But gentlemen, our friend Tobbh's explained it. It is the tomb of Hradzka, and it has been the tomb of Hradzka for ten thousand years before Hradzka was born!"

www.ingramcontent.com/pod-product-compliance
Lightning Source LLC
Chambersburg PA
CBHW032206190626
46810CB00018B/1877